Of Wilful Intent

The inhabitants of quiet, residential Lynden Grove were being driven to desperation by sporadic outbursts of teenage vandalism directed against their homes. The police seemed powerless to prevent it and were so anxious to avoid wrongful arrests that they leaned over backwards to be fair to the vandals. By the time Philip Butler's wife looked like losing her baby and perhaps her sanity as a result of the violence, the middle-class backlash was poised to strike.

When it did, the results were unexpected. Worse still, dissension broke out among the inhabitants of Lynden Grove as violence bred violence in an escalation of horror. By the time this brief, powerful novel reaches its stunning climax there are no winners, only losers, in this battle which encapsulates a tragedy of our times.

SHEILA JOHNSON

Of Wilful Intent

COLLINS, ST JAMES'S PLACE, LONDON

William Collins Sons & Co. Ltd
London · Glasgow · Sydney · Auckland
Toronto · Johannesburg

First published 1982
© Sheila Johnson 1982

British Library Cataloguing in Publication Data

Johnson, Sheila
    Of wilful intent. — (The Crime Club).
    I. Title
    823'.914 [F]   PR6060.0
    ISBN 0-00-231909-8

Photoset in Compugraphic Baskerville
Printed in Great Britain by
T. J. Press (Padstow) Ltd

CHAPTER 1

'What time is it?' Ann's voice was terse and high, betraying some of the tension behind the innocently posed question.

'What's that?' Philip carefully maintained his pretence of interest in the figures flickering across the television screen. 'Sorry, love. What did you say?'

'I asked what the time is.' Now there was a hint of frightened tears in her tone as Ann clasped and unclasped nervous fingers around the tiny matinée coat she was sewing. Philip dropped his show of concentration and reached over to take her shaking hands in his own.

'Don't get so worked up, darling. It's so bad for you, and bad for the baby. Remember what the doctor said — take everything easy.'

'Oh, Philip, I can't help it. It's getting worse all the time. We sit here, every weekend, just waiting, it's terrible. I don't think I can go on any more.'

'Hey, steady, darling. Steady. It's not as bad as all that, and anyway, they might not come again.'

'They will, Philip. You know they will. Oh, I know you pretend it doesn't worry you but —' Ann's words were drowned in a whoop and a crash from the road outside that realized her worst fears. She clutched convulsively at her husband's hands, her eyes wide with terror.

Philip Butler pulled his wife close against his chest, stroking her shining cap of night-black hair and making a soothing murmur. But his face was far from gentle as his anger grew, tightening the muscles along his lean jaw and lending a savage gleam to his mild, grey eyes. A further demented screech and a rending sound, followed closely by a chant of profane language, pulled him to his feet.

'Stay here, darling. Turn the TV up. I'm going after them.'

'No! Oh Philip, no.' Ann grabbed wildly at the sleeve of his sweater; the wool stretched and gaped under the strain as he tore himself away.

'It's no good, Ann. I'm not going to take any more.' He wrenched the door of their sitting-room open and she heard his angry footsteps crossing the hall to the front door. Even as it was opened a shower of stones and half-bricks smashed into the glass panel alongside and through the widening gap of the opening door, cutting into Philip's unprotected face and head.

'Philip!' Ann screamed his name as she pushed her cumbersome body upright, away from the padded embrace of the settee where she and Philip had been sitting. 'Phil.' She trod heavily into the hall as Philip reeled back, dazed and blinded. Blood poured from a gash over his right eye and his cheekbone was already swelling.

'It's all right, Ann. Get yourself away from here. Don't stand where they can see you.' He held one hand cupped to his face, and with the other pulled her back along the hallway to the door letting into the kitchen.

Like a pair of threatened children they cowered in the small tiled room, grateful for the added protection of the hastily closed door.

'Let me look. Let me see that eye.' Her personal fears pushed into the background, Ann turned her attention to her husband, the near-hysteria of a moment before dying completely as she saw his need. Towering six feet two in his stockinged feet, he was too tall for her to reach comfortably while he stood over her, and she clucked with impatience. 'Sit down, darling. Over here, near the sink. You'll need that bathing, I should think.' Pulling a stool from under the breakfast bar, she guided him to it and snatched up a clean tea-cloth to wipe away some of the blood. Her swift intake of breath as she saw the extent of the injury caused Philip to ask, 'How is it, love? Is it deep?'

'It's pretty bad, Phil. I'll need the first-aid kit. Hold this cloth — like so — while I get some lint.'

By the time Ann had swabbed the cut with antiseptic and fixed a wad of lint over it with a generous amount of sticking-plaster, the sounds of destruction had died away. The ensuing silence held a tremulous quality as if the residents of the neighbouring houses were holding their breaths, scarcely daring to trust its duration. A knock sounded at the Butler's front door, and glass crunched underfoot as Trevor and Dawn Austin, who lived in the house opposite, stepped through the mess of the hall and into the kitchen with all the familiarity of very close friendship.

'Are you all right?' Dawn asked the question, but both of them looked with concern towards Ann. She was in the seventh month of a very difficult pregnancy and they had sped across the road to check on her welfare as soon as it had been safe to do so. It wasn't until she gestured weakly in Philip's direction that their eyes dropped from her white face to take note of the figure slumped against the crimson-splashed sink unit.

'Christ, Phil!' Trevor stepped forward to grip his friend's shoulder. 'What happened? How bad is it?' His eyes swept the corn-blond hair, darkened now across the front by congealed blood, and water from Ann's wet hand.

'It's just a cut, Trevor . . . Nothing much . . . I . . . I went to the door and —'

'You bloody idiot!' Concern made Trevor speak angrily. 'Don't you know any better yet?'

'Leave it, Trev. Let it go.' Philip waved a deprecating hand. The blow to his head had left him feeling sick and dizzy, unable to cope with any argument.

'Do you need a doctor?' Dawn asked from her place by

the kitchen door.

'I think so, Dawn. I think that cut needs stitching.' Reaction began to set in and Ann's voice shook as she replied.

'Here. Come and sit down, you. I'll make us all a cup of tea, then Trevor can run Philip over to Casualty.' Dawn looked for confirmation from her husband and he nodded his agreement.

'Yes, Dawn's right. You must get off your feet, Ann. We'll give you a hand later to clear up the mess, so there's no need to get yourself into a tizzy.'

'Oh, Trevor. I'm so sick of all this.' Ann lowered herself carefully on to the chair Dawn proffered. 'Why can't they leave us alone? What have any of us done to deserve this sort of thing?'

The question went unanswered. It had been asked all too often among them to warrant a reply.

Dawn elected to stay with Ann while the men went off in Trevor's car to get Philip's wound attended to at the hospital. Her two young sons, Mark and David, were away overnight staying with her parents—a precaution she and Trevor had adopted shortly after this regular débâcle had begun. The attacks hadn't amounted to much more than petty annoyance at that time, but gradually they had assumed malicious overtones as garden beds were trampled and laid waste, windows smashed, and standing cars sprayed with corrosive acids or treated to a tankful of sand and gravel.

There had been a lot of discussion and argument, and a determined formation of a local tenants' association, in an attempt to find some way of preventing these forays, but as yet no one had come up with any solution, let alone any idea as to why their homes were being singled out for this destructive attention. The whole of their once pleasant neighbourhood had become affected, and neither appeals to the police nor their own attempts to lay hands on the gang responsible had succeeded in producing any deterrent.

Driving along the inner ring-road in the direction of the General Hospital, Trevor expounded his own carefully balanced theory to Philip. 'The way I see it,' he had begun, 'is like this: the root cause just has to be misguided jealousy. I mean, look at the sort of yobbos they are. Dirty, illiterate. Too stupid to hold down a job if they could get one—which most of them can't—so they see our places, know they'll never amount to more than two rooms in someone else's rented property at best, and consequently their resentment builds up until they come to take their spite out on us in the manner we've all come to know.'

Philip lifted his throbbing head and turned painfully to get a view of Trevor's bearded profile through his undamaged left eye. 'Y'know, Trev, you take the whole bloody thing far too calmly to suit me. Our homes, our wives and kids, our whole way of life is under siege and you can still cogitate on the whys and wherefores. Well, I'll tell you something. I'm not putting up with it any longer. If the police won't do anything about it, I bloody well will.'

'I don't see what there is for you to do, Phil,' came the placating reply. 'Unless you do the same as I intend to, and put your house up for sale.'

'You what?—You're not!—Aw, Trev: you're never going to knuckle under to those sodding villains!'

' 'Fraid so, old mate. I'm going down to the estate agents first thing on Monday morning. I'll take Dawn and the boys somewhere that I know will be free from this sort of bother.'

'Have you and Dawn talked it over, then? Made your minds up?'

'I've made *my* mind up. After tonight, I'm sure Dawn will agree.'

Philip squinted up at the resolute profile a second time. Don't be too sure of that, was his swift thought. But he was too fond of his friend to risk voicing his own private certainty that Dawn would not agree in the slightest.

A pert, freckle-faced nurse fastened a fresh zinc pad across the five neatly placed stitches over Philip's right eye and asked him if she could expect to do the same for the 'other fellow' later.

'If I had my way, love,' Philip told her grimly, 'you'd be sticking both his arms and legs into plaster of paris.'

The sunny smile faded and the nurse turned to tidy away the soiled dressing on the trolley without further comment. She had heard that note of suppressed anger in too many voices since she'd been working on the Casualty ward. These private vendettas made little sense to her when the end result made nothing but more work for an already overburdened medical team.

'Come on, Phil. Let's get you back home.' Trevor helped him into his jacket and smiled sympathetically at the girl. 'Don't worry, Nurse. He's not really the fighting sort,' he told her confidently.

By the time Trevor turned the car back into Lynden Grove, Philip was feeling decidedly ill. His head throbbed, his vision was blurred, and he was just keeping his fingers crossed that he would be able to get out of the car before he was violently sick.

'Oh no.' A low groan of protest escaped him as they drew up in front of his home and he saw a group of his neighbours milling around in the brightly lit interior.

Trevor, correctly guessing the cause of his inhospitable reaction, was quick to offer assistance. 'Don't worry, Phil. Once we've got you indoors and checked that Ann is okay, Dawn and I will shoo them all out. I expect they've only come round to offer their help.'

'Yes, I expect they have.' Philip was contrite as he heaved himself out of the car and started up the short driveway that led to his front door and the shattered remains of the glass-panelled hallway. The whole group of neighbours, most of them young marrieds like Ann and himself when they'd moved into the newly built houses six years ago, had proved more than generous with their help towards one another, whatever the need, and Philip acknowledged himself grateful. He was met at his front door by Sue, the female half of the Turner couple from next door at No. 10.

'Is Ann okay?' he asked, hurriedly forestalling her rush of outraged comment at the sight of his padded eye.

'Yes, don't worry, she's fine. We're just waiting for the police. George phoned them before we came round. Come and sit down, Phil. You look dreadful.'

The long through-lounge that was a feature of all the detached houses in the Grove seemed packed to capacity, but the crowd sorted itself out into just three couples, plus one unattached male, in addition to Ann and himself. Barry and June Simpson had come from No. 14, and Sue's husband George was there helping her dispense coffee. Dawn and Trevor made the last of the pairs, with the lone male, Graham Collins, from further along the Grove, completing the gathering.

'They've gone too far this time,' Graham said heavily. 'Wrecking property is one thing, but inflicting bodily harm is quite another. I've left Dorothy trying to quieten the kids; poor little beggars were scared stiff. I wouldn't have left them, but things are quiet now and I could see you needed help. It's got to be stopped, you know—all this. Before somebody gets killed.'

A murmur of agreement followed his words and was rumbling into a chorus of proposed action when a panda car drew up outside, guided to the house by the light streaming from its every window. Again, it was Sue Turner who went to open the door, and she returned to usher a police sergeant and a constable into the room. A babble of voices all attempted an answer in response to the sergeant's request for information, only to die away in embarrassed silence as he held up a broad hand.

'Sorry, folks, sorry. One at a time if you would,' he invited.

Trevor looked around at his neighbours, seeking their election as spokesman. At their nods of acquiescence he began explaining the situation. Then halted abruptly in mid-sentence. 'But you must know all this, Sergeant. Good heavens, we've made enough complaints about it.'

'Not me, sir. I'm new to this district — Sergeant Parker, just posted in on promotion. So why don't you begin right at the beginning and I'll take it from there.'

'Right you are, then.' Trevor drew a deep breath and recommenced his story. He spoke for some time without interruption, then the sergeant broke in to ask sharply:

'Nearly a year, you say, sir? Just a minute — Constable, have you got all that?' He turned to watch the young constable scribbling furiously in his notebook. The constable nodded but did not look up. 'And what generally happens then? What's the pattern?' The sergeant turned his attention back to Trevor.

'Well, it's always on a Saturday. Always about ten-thirty, eleven o'clock. The first we ever know about it is when they start to yell and swear. Then come the bangs and crashes and the clatter of feet pounding along the pavements as they tear through the Grove.'

'And is this *every* Saturday?'

'Oh no. It would be easy enough for you to catch them if it was. No.' Trevor paused to reflect. 'No, there is sometimes a gap of several weeks between the raids. Sometimes we don't even hear them. We just go out of doors the next morning congratulating ourselves that we've been given a miss, only to find our cars sprayed with battery acid or the contents of the dustbins strewn over our front lawns.'

'They completely smashed the goldfish pond from my front garden — I live at No. 6 — and then they shoved all the fish through the letter-box.' Graham felt moved to chip in. 'That was in the beginning, before we really knew what was going on. The kids found their fish all over the hall the next morning.'

'And you say this has all been reported before?' the sergeant asked him.

'Times,' came the despondent reply.

'And we've not caught up with any of them?'

'No, Sergeant. We had a constable assigned to a special beat along Lynden Grove and round the immediate area for some time, but they're not daft, those swine. They just wait for the fuss to die down, then start all over again.' Trevor resumed his role as spokesman.

'Can you give me a description of any of these, er, people?' the sergeant asked hopefully.

'Not really. They all wear jeans and leather jackets—the heavy black type—with loads of metal studs and fringeing. And either boots or clogs by the sounds of them. But the real outstanding thing about them is their headgear. You see, they all have those fancy balaclava type helmets that cover everything but their eyes.'

'Yes. And somebody must knit them specially,' said Ann with conviction, 'because although they are all a different colour they each have a big black vampire bat thing over the face part and the eye-holes are in the wings.'

'We've tried chasing after them—' George joined in the conversation now—'but they take off over the fields, running like hares.'

'Now let me get this straight in my mind,' the sergeant begged. 'Lynden Grove is the last road on the private estate, right?' Trevor nodded. 'And to one side, crossing the end of the Grove, is a lane—leading where?'

'It goes to Willowbank Farm. And from there it circles the old Saxon church before it leads into the village of Shipley,' George supplied.

'Right! So you have open fields to one side bordered by the lane, and also along the rear of the properties. What lies in the other direction?'

'The council estate. The main road divides this estate from the council estate. Lynden Grove leads into the main road at that end. Once you cross over you are on council property.'

'Hmm,' the sergeant looked thoughtful. 'Any pubs?'

'Two. One just the other side of the main road, about a hundred yards into the council estate. And the other at the back of the estate, about half a mile away.'

'And your troubles begin about chucking-out time, eh? Ten-thirty to eleven. Is that about right?'

'Yes, but we've checked at the pubs. The landlords swear they get no gangs on their premises. They have no trouble, it seems. And to be honest, the yobbos always come from the other end of the road. From the farm lane.'

'Then perhaps that's where we shall concentrate our efforts.' The sergeant turned towards the door as if his enquiries were concluded, and the constable finished his scribblings with a sigh of relief. 'Just leave things to us,' recommended the sergeant. 'Don't try tackling this sort of thing by yourselves, however much you would like to. Oh, by the way, about how many of them are there?'

'Nine, maybe ten.' Trevor glanced around for confirmation.

'Yes. That would be about right.' Philip supported his estimation. 'About ten. All seemingly tall, long-legged fellows. We've put them around their late teens, early twenties from what we've seen of them. Probably yobs from the tower blocks over on the estate.'

'That could be an unfair assumption, sir. If you don't mind my saying so.'

'In what way?' Philip demanded, bristling at the implied criticism.

'Well, one thing we've learned in this game—' the sergeant waved a hand to indicate the constable and himself—'is never to make assumptions. For example: you could assume they are all blacks, couldn't you? On account of the fact that they easily outdistance you when you give chase. I mean, *everyone* knows the black races are very good runners, seems like they have legs going right up to their shoulders.'

Philip lowered his angry one-eyed gaze feeling more than a little sheepish. The sergeant had put his finger unerringly on one of the suggestions they had all been guilty of making.

'On the other hand, they could be a gang of Pakistanis, couldn't they?' the sergeant went on. 'There is a large contingent of them not a hundred miles from here, and again *everyone* knows they are the ones fond of intricate design— like fancy knitted woollen hats and so on.' His measured glance raked them all in turn. No one made any attempt to argue with his logic. 'Well, I'll say good night to you now,' he said evenly. 'I'll be around some time tomorrow to get a look at the situation in daylight. So if in the meantime any of you can come up with any *facts* that might be of help, perhaps you will let me know?' His glance travelled over them all once again. But no one made any remark and he raised his hand in a farewell salute before stepping out into the night.

Nobody lingered after the policeman had left—there was a lot they were all eager to discuss, not least the sergeant's attitude—but they could see from Philip's face that he was about all-in, and Ann was also looking white and strained. George and Graham between them had fixed a sheet of asbestos, borrowed from Barry's embryo garage, over the shattered glass in the hall. The women had cleared away the mess, sweeping up the glass and stones, leaving behind only the coffee cups they had been using for Ann to wash in the morning. She and Philip bade their neighbours good night, coupled with grateful thanks, before they turned out the lights and climbed up to bed in silence, neither of them prepared to burden the other with a description of how ill they were feeling.

The pain in Philip's head was almost unbearable. He had been given a couple of tablets by the nurse at the hospital and had been handed on leaving one of the smallest packets he had ever laid eyes on.

'There are two more pain-killers in there, Mr Butler,' she had said in dismissal. 'But I'm sure you won't need them.'

He swallowed them now with a glass of water before sliding into bed beside his wife.

' 'Night, darling,' he said, pulling the bedclothes up over his shoulders.

' 'Night, love,' Ann replied through clenched teeth before reaching out to turn off the light.

CHAPTER 2

Neither of them managed to sleep. Philip lay back on his pillows and was buffeted into a throbbing half-world of semi-conscious dreams. By his side, and trying not to disturb what she imagined was a deep, healing sleep, Ann herself strove to get some rest. The weight of the baby was becoming increasingly burdensome, and the stabbing pains in her back and side prevented any serious hopes she might have held of getting a few hours' blessed relief in sleep. Miserably she sought to find an easy position for the bloated lump of her extended stomach. No matter how she turned or where she lay, the pains went on and the discomfort increased. A low groan escaped her, quickly stifled lest she should wake Philip. She struggled upright, dropping her legs over the side of the bed she attempted to stand. Her legs and feet, puffy with fluid, buckled beneath her, and she dropped to the floor with a spine-wrenching thud. She lay where she had fallen, gasping for breath, unable to make any move to ease her twisted position.

'Phil,' she called apologetically, hating to disturb his rest. 'Phil!' He made no response and she heard the deep snoring sound of his breathing continue uninterrupted. 'Philip!' This time desperation lifted her voice to a shout, but still she failed to rouse him. Weak tears of pain and fright started from her eyes as she squirmed around, trying her utmost to rise. Grasping the hanging bed-clothes, she tugged at them for support and cried in earnest as they slid towards her. 'Philip! Oh, Philip!' She was sobbing now, afraid for herself, afraid for her baby and afraid that her husband was deeply unconscious. How long she lay there she was never to know, but the pain and the cold and Philip's stentorian breathing dragged each second into hours. Finally, filling her lungs and throwing back her head, she screamed in a resounding, throat-tearing crescendo.

Dimly Philip registered the sound and clawed his way up towards consciousness. When he met the throbbing pain at the top of his skull, his overriding desire was to let go and return to the easy, comforting darkness. A second cry for help prevented it.

He struggled on, fighting to open his eyes, running an oversized tongue round a furry cavern that had once been his mouth. The saliva began to flow, a bitter-tasting glue that set him coughing and choking into full awareness.

'Ann.' His flailing hand encountered the empty place beside him, discovered the absence of both his wife and the bedclothes. 'Ann, darling?' He sat up, wincing as the sudden movement sent shafts of pain knifing through his head.

'Philip.' The timorous voice rising from below the level of the bed brought him to his feet, and sent him stagger-ing around the bed in shambling haste. His hand groped out, finding the light switch as he passed, and the room leapt into focus.

Ann! Oh my God! Ann.' All concern with his own misery was swept away as he dropped to his knees at her side. 'Darling, what is it? What are you doing here? Why didn't —'

'Help me, Philip. Help me.' Her hand came up in desperate appeal, stopping the words in his throat. 'Get the doctor, love. Oh, please. Get the doctor here quickly.'

'Let me lift you back into bed first.' He slid his arms beneath her, but was halted by her sharp cry of pain.

'No, Phil. Don't. Just get the doctor,' she begged, her head rolling from side to side in her agony.

Philip stumbled from the room and fled down the stairs, bouncing from the wall to the banister and back again as his limited vision failed to accommodate his need for speed. He grabbed the phone from its rest and was already dialling the numbers when he realized he was getting no dialling tone. Cursing fluently, he jiggled the rests, willing the unresponsive instrument to answer to his demands. Seconds dragged into years as his impatience mounted. Flinging the receiver back on to the cradle, he started towards the front door, recollected himself and turned to retrace his footsteps as far as the foot of the stairs, where he called reassuringly up to Ann: 'I won't be a second, darling. The phone's dead. Just try to hang on; I'm going across the road to use Trevor's.' He didn't wait to hear if she made any reply, but started off out of the house and across the road without pausing even to put a coat over his pyjamas.

Hammering at the front door of No. 11 he resolved that whatever the outcome of this night's work, he was going to put an end to the current reign of spite and destruction, even if he had to break a few necks to do it. Be they white, red *or* black!

The door was pulled from under his pounding fist by a

very bleary-eyed Trevor.

'Philip! What the hell's going on?'

'It's Ann. She's bad and our phone isn't working.'

'Come in then, come in.' Trevor pulled him through the hall to the lounge, where the telephone sat on a corner table. 'There, help yourself. Do you know the number?'

'Yeah, thanks. I've learned it by heart since Ann's been pregnant.' Philip began dialling as Trevor turned to explain the situation to Dawn who had trailed into the room.

She waited while Philip reached the emergency service and made his request for help before she spoke. 'Would you like me to come across with you? I'm no great shakes at first aid or anything. But if I can be of any help . . .' Her face as much as her words conveyed her genuine concern.

'I'd be grateful if you would, Dawn,' Philip said, and meant it. 'I don't know what to do for the best.'

The doctor arrived within twenty minutes. Luckily, he was one of the team from their local surgery that had been monitoring the progress of Ann's pregnancy, so there was no delay while he checked her case history. Nor did he waste any time exclaiming over the obvious damage to their property or Philip's face until he had examined Ann, given her a calming injection and availed himself of Dawn's telephone to call for an ambulance.

'Now then,' he said, perching himself on the side of the bed and addressing Philip. 'Perhaps I'd better take a look at you while I'm here.'

'There's no need, Doctor. I had my eye stitched at the hospital only last night, so I'm okay.'

'Hmm.' The doctor reached over to fish through his bag and brought out a pencil-light which he flicked on and off before getting to his feet and motioning Philip to come closer. Philip gave in with a shrug and submitted to having the light flashed into his good eye from a variety of angles. 'Ye-es. Uh-uh. Just as I thought. A mild concussion. Some delay in your reflexes. Got a headache, have you? Hmm, yes. Better come for a check-up first thing Monday morning. Don't want the two of you crocked up, do we now?'

'Aw, I'm all right,' Philip began, but a small sound of protest from Ann drew him to kneel by her side, his objections forgotten.

'Do . . . do as he asks, darling, please,' Ann begged softly.

'All right, darling. All right. Just you hang in there. Everything will be fine.'

'The ambulance is here.' Dawn had come up the stairs to inform them, and the doctor went down with her to direct the men with the stretcher.

'Are you going with her?' Dawn asked, eyeing Philip's pyjama-clad legs, which showed below the Paisley-patterned dressing-gown he'd dragged on while they'd been waiting for the doctor.

'I think perhaps not.' The doctor looked steadily into Philip's face. 'There's nothing you can do for her if you go. The baby is not going to put in an appearance for several weeks yet. I just want your wife in hospital as a precaution, Mr Butler. She's in no danger, believe me.'

'But I can't just leave her,' Philip protested as the men negotiated the stairs with Ann on the stretcher between them.

'She's in very good hands, rest assured. And she'll probably sleep for several hours until the effects of the injection wear off. It would be better all round if you could do the same. You can visit tomorrow.'

'Come on, Philip. No sense in making yourself ill.' Dawn placed a sympathetic hand on his arm. 'Go and get some rest, then come across in the morning to ring the hospital, eh?'

'We-ell—only if you're sure she won't need me.' His good eye pleaded for assurance from the doctor, who gave it in full measure, and the three of them stood together in the road as the ambulance, with Ann on board, pulled quietly away.

Philip slept heavily, only awakening at the sound of the rain drumming loudly against the window. He sat up, pawing groggily at his face. The zinc pad under his fingers brought the events of the previous night rushing back. What time was it? He snatched up the alarm clock and moaned aloud when he read the digital figures. Ten fifty-six. God, he'd slept the morning away, and he'd meant to be at the hospital as early as possible. He stumbled into the bathroom, cut himself a couple of times shaving, and was dragging on his shirt when he heard Dawn calling up the stairs.

'I hope you're decent. I've brought you some breakfast.'

He stepped out on to the landing, fingers still clumsily struggling to fasten shirt buttons.

'I've phoned the hospital. Ann is fine. You can visit any time after two o'clock.'

'Dawn, you're an angel. What did they say exactly? Did they give you any idea what she—'

'They told me only that she is comfortable, and that you can see her later. Here, get yourself outside of this while I make some coffee.' Dawn handed him a covered tray as he reached the lowest tread of the stairs, and hurried into the kitchen. Philip followed more slowly, still only half awake. 'Trevor says he'll drive you over to the hospital. You can hardly manage yourself with only one eye and a peppermint, can you?' She gave him a warm smile. 'How is the eye this morning, anyway?'

Philip blinked vigorously and managed a grin. 'D'you know, I hate to admit it, but I haven't really had time to find out yet.'

'No, I don't suppose you have. We were watching for you to open the bedroom curtains before I came across, we didn't want to wake you.' She turned to switch off the kettle and pour the boiling water on to the instant coffee. 'I'll leave you in peace now to get on with your breakfast. Come across as soon as you're ready.'

'Thanks, Dawn. Thanks a lot.' Philip eyed the loaded tray with something akin to dismay. The last thing in the world he wanted was food, and Dawn had prepared the meal with a lavish hand. He sipped at the scalding coffee, then pushed the tray away and sprang to his feet. He couldn't just sit around. He wanted to speak to the hospital, to find out for himself that Ann was all right. He was half way to the front door before the basic instincts of civility halted his stride. He couldn't go charging across the road demanding the use of his friend's telephone, leaving a meal prepared with the best of intentions to congeal on the kitchen table. He reached out and caught at the newel-post at the foot of the stairs, his fingers grasping and kneading at the painted wood as he fought down his agitation. The hall was steeped in unaccustomed gloom, the sheet of asbestos tacked in place of the broken glass panel cutting out most of the daylight. God, what a shambles. His despairing eye noted several tears and dirty streaks on the once immaculate wallpaper, and he added the chore of redecorating to the growing list of repairs. Turning his back on the wreckage, he wandered through into the kitchen, where he scraped the now cold bacon and eggs on to a sheet of newspaper, adding the contents of the toast-rack before making a careful parcel which he carried out to the dustbin. No sense in leaving the evidence for Dawn to discover. This way he'd avoid any hurt to her feelings. Having paced impatiently for the minimum length of time he could safely have allotted to eating the meal, he collected the clean crockery together and headed for the house over the road.

'Well, that didn't take you long,' Dawn commented as she opened the door to him.

'No, it was delicious, Dawn. And I was starving. Can I use the phone?'

Philip slid hurriedly over the lie, making great play of brushing the rain from his shoulders, unwilling to meet Dawn's appraising eye.

'Course you can. Go on through.' Dawn took the tray and left him alone to make his call.

The response from the hospital was disturbing. A female voice, after enquiring his name, advised him to hold on and was replaced by another, slightly brisker tone. This time Philip was told to ask for a Dr Osborne on his visit to the hospital.

'I should come a little before visiting time, Mr Butler. Then you will catch the doctor before he leaves.'

'Can you tell me what it's about?' Philip asked, alarm rising in him. 'I mean, how is she? — My wife. Is everything all right with her? With the baby?'

'Please, Mr Butler. It would be much better for you to save all these questions until you see the doctor.'

'But—' Philip began to argue.

'This afternoon . . . about one-thirty. I'm sure Dr Osborne will be able to answer all your questions then. Goodbye, Mr Butler.' The voice was not unkindly, but it was certainly firm, and Philip found himself staring stupidly at the silent telephone receiver as the conversation was politely terminated. He dropped it back into its cradle and went in search of Dawn and Trevor.

They were sitting at the breakfast-table drinking coffee, their eyes fastened on his face as he entered the kitchen.

'How is she?' Dawn asked hesitantly, reading the worst into his worried expression.

'They didn't say. Well, not really. They want me to see a Dr Osborne, about half past one. Will that be okay,

Trevor? I mean, I can take my car if it's going to muck up your day running me about.'

' 'Sno trouble, Phil. Honestly.' Trevor spoke sincerely. ' 'Sides, I doubt if that old banger of yours would manage without its weekend rest,' he said in an attempt to introduce a lighter tone.

'No, you're right there,' Philip agreed somewhat ruefully. 'Still, it'll have to last a bit longer for all that. Every time I get a bit put by and start to think of trading her in, something else comes along to take it. Now that Ann isn't working things get a bit tight.' He pulled a sour face. 'And I can do without all this additional aggro. I tell you straight, Trev. I'm not going to put up with much more.'

'Do same as us then,' said his friend enigmatically.

'What? Move out, you mean?'

'Oh no, Trevor.' Dawn rounded on her husband. 'We're not going to move out.'

'It's the only thing to do, love,' he said patiently. 'You must see that. We can't go on in this fashion, sending the boys to your mum's every weekend, living in continual cycles of war and peace, it just isn't on.'

'I don't care! I'm not going to let those . . . those . . . I'm not going to be driven out of my home.' Dawn's eyes blazed and Philip, glancing from her angry face, saw Trevor lower his eyes and was suddenly aware that he had deliberately waited until they had his company before voicing his proposal. Well, I'll be blowed, was his surprised thought. So that's how the land lies, old Trev's half afraid of her.

'And who do you think will buy this place, then?' The disgust ringing in Dawn's voice brought Philip's attention back to the threatened quarrel. 'Do you think folk are all fools, or are you hoping no one will let on?'

Trevor shrugged helplessly as his wife's anger broke over him. 'Oh, let it go, Dawn. We'll talk it over when you've had time to think about it.'

'Oh no we won't! We'll talk about it now. And Philip is just as involved as we are, so don't think to make him an excuse for putting it off,' said Dawn with the swift insight of a woman who knows her man. 'In any case, I can't think for the life of me why you men don't all get together and give those sods a bloody good hammering.'

'Wish it was as easy as that, Dawn,' Philip put in with a wry grimace, feeling a little guilty at leaving his friend to bear the brunt of this prod of inadequacy. 'I'd like nothing better, and so would the rest of us, but it's catching them — as you very well know,' he added, hoping to draw the sting from her anger.

His ploy was successful, for Dawn heaved a sigh before muttering in a more controlled manner, 'Yes . . . Well. It's time something was done, and I don't see why we should be pushed into running away.'

The subject was then allowed to drop, and the men switched to the safe discussion of yesterday's football matches until it was time to leave for the hospital. Philip's anxiety mounted as they squeezed into the last remaining space in the car park and climbed out to face the sprawling old buildings that sheltered the city's sick and infirm.

Finding the right ward was an art in itself, but a series of enquiries led them along the endless green-painted corridors until they reached the glass-sided office heading the room where Ann had been admitted.

'I'll, er, I'll wait in the corridor.' Trevor ducked back through the doorway, leaving Philip to approach the white-clad figures inside.

'Dr Osborne?' he asked of the only male, and was relieved when the tired-looking man rose from his seat.

'Yes. I'm Dr Osborne. You'll be Mrs Butler's husband, I take it?' At Philip's nod he motioned him further inside the small office. 'Thank you, Sister,' he nodded in dismissal of his two female colleagues. As they left the office he again turned to Philip. Plucking his upper lip between his finger and thumb, he tugged absently as he studied the bandaged face.

'Your wife is in an acute state of distress,' he stated without preamble. 'There is also some renal failure. I shall need your signature for a Cæsarean.' He looked at Philip accusingly. 'But I didn't get you here today for that. I'll tell you frankly, I'm worried about her mental state. What has been going on to bring her to this pass?'

Philip experienced the same defensive confusion that used to accompany his visits to his headmaster's office when he was a boy. He opened his mouth to protest and, so intense was the sensation, he almost prefaced his remarks with the customary 'Please, sir,' of those long-ago days. Starting slowly and choosing his words with care, he told the doctor at some length of the Saturday-night raids, and ended by saying lamely, 'There is nothing I can do about it.'

'Have you thought about moving? Or at least moving your wife out for a time? Back to her parents, perhaps.'

'We can't afford to move. It took every penny we had to get that place. And both Ann's parents are dead.'

'I see. That's a great pity in more ways than one. They could possibly have been the best ones to help at this time.' He paused thoughtfully, then returned to the attack. 'And so. What happens when the child arrives? Do you hope to give it a normal upbringing in your present circumstances?'

'I've thought till I'm sick.' Philip spread helpless hands. 'What can I do? I've been to the law, they don't seem to do anything.'

'Hmm.' The doctor rubbed his hands over his face, be-traying nights without proper sleep. He had softened vis-ibly as Philip's story progressed, and he blinked at him now with a certain compassion. 'It's a strange world we're living in, I'm afraid, when one half of society seeks to destroy the life and property of the other. The whys and wherefores of such behaviour escape me, *but—*' the word rang out as his voice took on determination— 'our immediate problem is your wife. She has to be our first concern. Now, I suggest you go in there and give her all the comfort you can. What you say to her is your business, but lie through your back teeth if you have to. I want her brought to a much happier frame of mind before I attempt the Cæsar.'

'What are her chances, Doctor? I mean . . . is she . . . is there . . . ?' Philip floundered, unable to voice his fears.

The doctor tugged again at his upper lip. 'Physically,' he offered at last, 'we should pull her through. And the child. The rest depends on how much reassurance you are able to give her.' His gaze left Philip in no doubt of his meaning.

CHAPTER 3

The journey home from the hospital was completed in silence. After taking one look at his friend's set face Trevor had made no attempt at conversation beyond his first anxious enquiry regarding Ann's condition. He could see Philip was wrestling with some pretty dark thoughts and he left him to them. He drove steadily and carefully through the Sunday afternoon traffic. The windscreen-wipers swept to and fro, beating their measured tattoo, counting off the miles and then the yards until he turned into his own front drive and dragged at the hand-brake, bringing it into place with a grating click-click-click that seemed perversely to release Philip's tongue.

'She's so tiny, Trev. So . . . So . . .' Philip spread his hands, aware of his inadequacy to express what he was feeling. The picture of Ann, her dark hair making the pale, strained face seem even whiter against the starched

hospital pillow, swam before his eyes. God! The last hour
had been bloody grim. He'd gone bouncing into the three-
bedded ward playing the happy expectant father for all
he was worth. The sweat started from his temples as he
recalled the lies he'd spooned out like heavy syrup. The
gang had been caught, he'd told her. Last night while he
and Dawn had been waiting for the ambulance to come.
He'd seen the police sergeant this very morning before he
came along to the hospital. No more Saturday night
raids, he'd promised her glibly. No more trouble. No
more smashed windows or broken fences. No more nights
spent just waiting for them to tear their houses down
around their ears. They were just kids . . . hadn't realized
the heartache they were causing . . . but they were all
sorry now.

'Just wait,' he'd gone on, embroidering his tale. 'It'll be
so blooming quiet now we'll have to kick a few cans about
just to make sure we're still alive.' The eye? Oh, that!
That was nothing, nearly better. He'd have the padding
off before he came back tomorrow. Of course he was
going in to work. After he'd done as their doctor had
asked and had a quick check-up, he'd added hastily as her
face again betrayed her anxiety. All she had to do now
was rest, and think about the baby. She'd be holding him
in her arms soon, their son and heir, that was something
to look forward to, wasn't it? He'd held his wide grin until
the muscles in his face felt as though they would crack.
Come on, sweetheart. Buck up. His mind kept repeating
the words as though by his very insistence they would
produce the desired effect. And all the while he had
known of the ordeal that was facing her. The Cæsarean
operation that hadn't been mentioned to her yet, and the
raids that would probably go on and on, terrifying her,
driving her towards inevitable breakdown.

'I'm going to stop them,' he said now to Trevor, who
knew what he meant without further elaboration. Neither

man made any move to get out of the car. Philip's voice rang with conviction. 'It only has to be done once. Dawn was right. There are enough men living along the Grove to give those hooligans the pasting they deserve.'

'And how do you propose going about it?'

'It's simple. I don't know why we've never thought of it before. Look.' Philip turned and pointed along the road. 'That's where they come from, the fields.' He twisted in his seat. 'And that's where they go. All along the Grove inflicting their damage, and out the other end. Now, all we have to do is get all the men together, divide them into two groups, one to each end of the Grove, then wait. Let the yobbos get started along the road, then close in from each end. We'll trap them between us.'

'And then what? You can't seriously suggest that we duff them up.'

'Why not? Haven't they done us all enough harm between them? I tell you it's the only way, Trev. Give them a taste of their own medicine.'

'You know, you're as bad as Dawn.' Trevor tried a smile, he appreciated the strain his friend was under and had no wish to quarrel with him, but really, this was going just a little too far.

'I'm serious, Trevor. If you want out, just say so. But I'm going to see what the rest of the blokes have to say.' Philip pushed the car door open and swung his legs out. 'I'll go along the row now to see who's at home. I'm going to ask them all to come round to my place Monday night, or Tuesday—whichever seems best. I'll get some beer in and we'll get things planned properly.'

Trevor sat behind the steering-wheel, thoughtfully contemplating the rain pouring down the bright yellow paint of his garage door.

'Well?' Philip's word jerked at him.

'Okay, okay. Let's check with the others, then. I'll take this side, you take the other,' he said on a resigned sigh.

'Better make it for Tuesday, just in case we don't catch them all in today,' he added without enthusiasm.

Both of them were soaked to the skin, and it was fast approaching the time for Philip to return to the hospital for the evening visiting hour, before they had completed their calls on their neighbours. Dawn was waiting impatiently under the shelter of the front porch for each of them to emerge from the houses she had last seen them approaching.

'Come along with you,' she chided, catching sight of Philip at last. 'Come and have a hot bath and get into some dry clothes before you catch your death. You too,' she scolded Trevor as he dashed through the puddles along the front drive. 'It's a pity you haven't both got more sense.' She was a tall girl and well-rounded. She would be what is more kindly known as 'a big woman' when she got to middle age, and even now in her youth her proportions lent her unquestioned authority. The two men glanced sheepishly at each other's dripping clothes while she continued to berate them. Sensing their drawing together, she stopped her tirade and asked in more amiable tones, 'Well, who's to be first in the bath while I get you some tea ready?'

Philip had earlier refused lunch on the pretext of having just swallowed his breakfast. Now he found he was hungry. 'I'll run a bath for myself at home, Dawn. There's a boiler full of hot water, but I'd appreciate a sandwich or something before I go back to see Ann.'

'Then go and get on with it. And I'll have you something on the table by the time you're through,' she promised him.

Trevor and Dawn dropped Philip off at the hospital on their way out to collect their two boys. They offered to call back for him later, but he wouldn't hear of it, there was a reasonable bus service out to their estate and he felt indebted enough for all the help they had given him through the day. He found Ann looking a little brighter, despite having been warned of the impending operation.

'I don't really mind, Phil. Not if it means a better chance for the baby . . . And it will mean a whole lot less waiting, won't it?' she said.

'Yes, love, it will. Why, he'll be riding his first bike by Christmas,' Philip teased. 'Be needing a pair of football boots too, I shouldn't wonder.'

Ann could never be persuaded to accept Philip's confident expectations of a boy child, and had persisted in using the all-embracing 'it' whenever she spoke of the baby, but she smiled at him now, amused at his persistence.

'When, er . . . when do they . . . When is to be? The operation, I mean?'

'Tuesday. In the morning. I have to stay wired up to this thing until then.' She indicated the tubes in her left arm with a nod of her head.

'Do they hurt?'

'Not really. And anyway, it's not for long. Just the day after tomorrow.' She tightened her grip on his right hand. 'It's not like I thought it would be,' she said in a small voice that betrayed her unease. 'No midnight dash through the streets in a taxi with you half-dressed and frantic and me all cool and serene.'

Philip understood the effort her little joke cost, and blessed her for trying. He raised her hand to his lips and kissed it softly. 'It'll be all right, love,' he assured her. They had neither of them intended he should be present at the birth, which was just as well since it was now going to be impossible, but he was greatly reluctant to leave her. When they had talked about it, way back in the beginning when they had first learned Ann was pregnant, Philip had suggested he should stay with her right through, but she had protested vehemently.

'No, Phil. Never,' she had said flatly. 'You are the last person I want to see me like that.'

'See you like that? Don't be silly, darling. I thought — well, I thought you'd want me to be there.'

'Well, I don't. In fact, the very thought of it embarrasses me.'

'Oh darling, come on. You can't really mean that.'

'Yes. Yes, I do. I mean it, Philip. I think it's a revolting idea.'

'But isn't it what all the doctors recommend? I mean, isn't it supposed to create a closer bond between us all — you, me *and* the baby?'

'Rubbish! It's just that some men have a driving curiosity about something they can never experience for themselves. Come on, Philip. Admit it. What else would you want to be there for?'

'I thought maybe it would help you, make you feel better.' Philip pressed the point, but his voice lacked conviction.

'And you can stop me feeling pain then, can you?' Ann had pulled a wry mouth. 'There are still some little mysteries best left between man and woman, love. And I for one prefer it that way, thank you.'

Philip recalled their conversation now as he sat holding Ann's hands, miserably aware how inadequately equipped he was to spare her any of the ordeal that lay ahead. All he could do was tell her over and over again that he loved her, and always would.

True to his promise, Philip went along to the local surgery for a check-up on Monday morning. Lacking an appointment, he had to wait a considerable time before one of the doctors was free to see him, and then he was obliged to go through the whole story behind his injury for the benefit of the duty doctor who had no prior information regarding Philip's visit. He listened to the hasty explanation with raised brows.

'Do you tell me this is an accepted state of affairs Mr — ah, Butler?' he asked as the story came to an end.

'Here, in an ordinary, English town, there are people—householders—being harassed by a group of thugs in this manner?'

' 'Fraid so,' Philip confirmed.

'But surely something can be done? Why haven't they been stopped? Honestly, I find this most difficult to believe.' The doctor could have spared himself the speech; his incredulous expression told Philip all that he was saying—and a great deal more, which he was not. What are you afraid of? Why haven't you done something about it? Why do you sit back and accept it? were only some of the questions hanging in the antiseptic-laden air of the small consulting-room, and Philip was hard pushed to contain his temper.

'It's not simply a question of lying down to be kicked, you know, Doctor,' he said tightly. 'I've tried—We've all tried—to get hold of these bastards, but it's easier said than done.' He unclenched his fists and drew a steadying breath; this wasn't the doctor's problem, after all. 'Anyway, the important thing now is to get all this padding off my face, it's worrying my wife,' he said, attempting to get the subject dropped.

'Let me have a look at you, then. Mmm.' Cool fingers peeled away the dressing. 'That looks rather nasty. You shouldn't really leave it uncovered, you know. But if you insist I'll give you some ointment to put into the eye, and I would suggest you bathe it frequently until the inflammation goes down.' He pressed gently round the cheekbone and over the brow. 'I suppose you are aware that had it struck just a fraction lower, that brick or whatever it was would have taken your eye out.' Philip flinched as the probing fingers discovered a bruise on the side of his head. 'Tell me, do these vandals you speak of always draw blood?'

'No, thank God! Although this isn't the first time—oh, not me, it's the first time for me,' he added hastily as the doctor's face registered his incredulous amazement. 'But some months ago, before we realized how vicious things were becoming, they went along the Grove one night lifting all the gates from the hinges and propping them up to look as though they were still hanging. It was quite amusing at first. My next-door neighbour pulled his open and fell base over apex among his petunias.' Philip watched the doctor's smile broaden, then he went on, 'Next to fall for the joke—literally—was the wife of a chap further down the road. She wasn't so lucky. The gate fell on her and part of the wrought-iron fancy work embedded itself in her thigh. We couldn't get her free until they sent a doctor along to cut into her leg.'

Philip's check-up had been completed in a stunned silence. He was given a prescription for eye ointment and a sick-note to cover him for a week's absence from work. He'd been about to decline the latter, but when he thought about the difficulties of getting to and from the office without using his car, coupled with his desire to get the hall fixed up before Ann came home with the baby, he'd accepted without further ado. Didn't he spend his working life paying out state benefit to people far less justified in calling themselves unfit for work than he was at present, he asked himself grimly as he tucked the slip of paper into his pocket.

Contrary to Philip's confident prediction over the previous months, his son and heir was a girl. And a very sick little girl at that. The Cæsarean went ahead as planned at ten o'clock on Tuesday morning and he hovered anxiously outside the operating theatre praying alternatively for Ann and their child. Ann had been noticeably comforted by his vehement assurance that the threat they had been living under for so long was now a thing of the past. And his breezy assertions about the greatly improved state of his eye did much to put her mind at ease, but the gynæcologist had remained somewhat pessimistic regarding her condition.

'She is going to need all your support and constant affection, plus a complete absence of any form of mental stress for the next few months,' he had warned Philip. 'I'll do all I can for her, of course. But the real burden will fall on you, I'm afraid.'

A sudden flurry of movement called Philip back from his contemplation of that advice. There were sounds of approaching footsteps, and the swing-doors were banged apart by the nurse guiding a trolley. She nodded at Philip, who hurriedly crossed the room to her side. Ann was barely awake. Philip bent to kiss her forehead.

'It's a girl,' she whispered. 'Lit — little — girl.' She was drifting back to sleep under the effect of the anæsthetic, but she raised a limp hand to indicate the white-gowned figure emerging through the same swing-doors she herself had just been wheeled through. As the figure drew level, and the portable incubator was manoeuvred around the trolley Ann was lying on, Philip dropped his gaze to peer into the glass-sided box. A package of silver foil with tubes leading from it was all he was able to take in.

'You come along with your wife now, Mr Butler,' the nurse urged him. 'Then you can go through to the Prem. Baby Unit and make your daughter's acquaintance a little later.'

Philip did as he was bid, but a sick premonition clutched at his throat as he gazed down on Ann. If their baby was to die, what would the loss do to her, in her present delicately balanced mental state?

It was only later, when he'd had a chance to really look at the child, that he decided perhaps it would be something of a blessing if the fight for its life were to be lost. Staring at the baby through the tears flooding his already impaired vision, he felt a desperate urge to scream out against the Fates that had saddled him with this, their latest depraved jest. The head, lolling atop the minuscule body and limbs, seemed to him grotesquely huge. The tiny chest heaving and straining under the stress of drawing air into the lungs, was so distorted in its labours as to be inhuman. Only the hands, incredibly small but perfectly formed, the fingers starring in mute appeal as they rubbed again and again at the stocking hat covering the dome of the head, substantiated the claim that this creature was indeed the seed of his body.

Unable to bear any more of the laboured heaving for breath, Philip turned away and blundered out through the door of the unit into the glass-walled corridor. What had they told Ann? What could *he* tell Ann? And which would cause her the least grief—to lose the child now, before it ever really came into being, or to spend the rest of her life watching over and caring for this subhuman existence? Philip was racked with pent-up grief. He paced the corridor, beating one fist into the other, blind to all but his own abject distress. It was there the pædiatrician came upon him. Seeing the state he was in, and wrongly attributing its cause, the professional man hastened to offer reassurance.

'Don't give up hope so soon in the game,' he said. 'They're tough little blighters for all they're so tiny.'

Philip stared at him dully. That was precisely what he was now most afraid of.

'You are the Butler baby's father, I take it?' Calm green eyes studied the bruised face and the tightly clenched fists.

Philip nodded.

'Then you should have nothing to worry about. Your wife is fine and the baby is going to make it.'

Philip glared at him, accusation and rejection trembling on his lips. What did this complacent idiot know about it? No doubt his kids—if he had any—were just as they should be.

The glare was acknowledged and this time correctly interpreted. A surge of sympathy warmed the green eyes. 'Come with me.' He beckoned Philip to follow as he entered the Baby Unit. Philip hesitated. He had no wish to torture himself further by looking again at the grotesque contents of the nearest incubator. 'Come!' This time the voice held a note of command and Philip trod reluctantly forwards.

Ignoring the incubator marked 'BUTLER', his mentor passed along the unit to halt at the incubator farthest from the door. 'Now, look at this child,' he invited. Philip obediently looked at a rather small but quite unremarkable baby boy. He raised questioning eyes. 'This child weighed in at three pounds two ounces. He's now four pounds ten. When his weight reaches five pounds his mother will take him home.' They passed up the unit to the next incubator. Another boy. 'This one weighed four pounds two ounces at birth. He also had jaundice. We expect to send him home before the weekend.' This baby too looked perfectly normal to Philip.

The next child was a girl. She was smaller than either of the boys. 'This young lady weighed two pounds fourteen ounces at birth. She's now just a pound heavier. See how the head still looks a little too large for her body?' The question was asked casually without emphasis. They passed to the next incubator.

'Now, this boy is just three days old. He weighed in at two pounds ten ounces, the same as your child. He's lost two ounces since birth, but has now stabilized and we expect him to show a weight gain by tomorrow.' Philip found himself looking at a child as deformed as his own. Here was the grotesquely sized head, the string-like limbs and the protruding stomach. He turned to the doctor, his eyes asking the question his lips were unable to form.

'Not very pretty as yet, is he?' came the response. 'But he'll fill out, given time.' They came to the last incubator.

'And here, of course, is the Butler baby.' The doctor smiled briefly. 'She's not very pretty either at the moment, and her breathing is giving us a little concern. But I will rectify that when the nurse brings in the necessary equipment.' He paused reflectively, then went on in the same conversational tone. 'I expect she'll need some help over the next couple of days, but we have everything to hand here, as you can see, and time will take care of the rest, Daddy Butler. Of that you can rest assured.' He looked straight into Philip's face, and Philip, after swallowing deeply, held out his hand.

'Thank you,' he said simply. 'Thank you very much indeed.'

CHAPTER 4

There were twelve detached houses and sixteen semis along the length of Lynden Grove, standing four semis a side at either end with the twelve detached houses between them. There had been few changes of ownership since they were built; consequently the residents were all pretty much aware of one another's circumstances. With the exception of No. 21, where the young schoolteacher husband had packed his bags and departed some months ago, and No. 4, where Brian Goss was recovering from the effects of a road accident, every one of the homes was represented by an adult male at the meeting Philip had called for Tuesday evening. They had tried getting together before over this very same problem, usually in the local pub, but their wives had accompanied them on those occasions, lifting the otherwise serious business to a more social and festive plane. Now there were grim and determined faces among the twenty-six men that went oddly with the tobacco smoke and beer fumes thickening the atmosphere of the crowded room.

Most of them supported Philip's determination to bring retribution to the hooligans, although not all of them went along with his angrily declared intention of inflicting as much pain as possible in the process. To some, it was a bit of a game. Not that it wasn't a serious business, they hastened to assure one another, but the thought of lying in wait through the dark evening, then pouncing on their unsuspecting quarry, held the thrill of excitement they usually experienced only at second hand via their television sets.

'Do we arm ourselves? I mean, shall I bring the poker or something?' The speaker's face was alight with anticipation.

'Christ, no!' Trevor's emphatic and serious censure brought heads turning in his direction. 'We don't want a blood-bath. Just catch them and turn them over to the police,' he advised cautiously.

'Stuff that.' George Turner rounded on him. 'I'm having my pound of flesh, given the chance.' His words were greeted with sounds of laughing approval.

'Well, I'm not going to slap their legs and tell them to be good boys in future, either,' put in another.

'No bloody fear,' came the comment from someone at the back of the room. 'Let's give it to 'em proper once we've got 'em.'

'Wait! Just a minute, just a minute.' Trevor raised his voice to a shout and waved his arms to get their attention. As the mutters and laughter died away he looked around at the wall of bodies. He was of less than average height and was having difficulty seeing over the heads of his nearest neighbours.

'Here, climb up on this.' Someone thrust a footstool towards him and he stepped up, thankful for the advantage of the extra inches. That was better, now he could see them all. His spaniel-brown eyes were thoughtful as he took note of their impatient glances, and he was aware that unless he spoke up on the side of sanity the whole business could rapidly get out of hand. Running a nervous hand round his neatly trimmed beard, he began putting his case.

'Now please, just hear me out,' he begged, aware that not all he was going to say would find receptive ears. 'I'm just as anxious as any of you to put a stop to these vandals, but can't you see that if we turn to violence we'll be as bad as the creatures we are trying to bring down? We can't just go out on the streets and practise mob law. We've got to deal with this in a sensible manner—'

'Oh yeah? And where has that got us so far?' asked a disparaging voice, which immediately found support from half a dozen throats.

'That's right!'

'That's true! It's got us no-bloody-where.'

'Can't deal sensibly with maniacs, Trev.'

'Punch their bloody heads in, I say.'

'All right. Okay.' Trevor raised a quietening hand. 'But if we go out there with—with pokers and stuff, somebody is going to get killed.' He paused as his words induced a momentary silence. 'And let's face it, lads. They're not worth all the aggro that would give us.'

'Then what's the alternative?' Philip questioned his friend. 'I can't see them letting us round them up like a flock of lost sheep.'

'Maybe not, but look at us, man. There are over twenty able-bodied men right here in this room. Are we to go out there armed to the teeth with pokers and pick-handles to round up a bunch of kids? That *would* give them kudos, wouldn't it? Even if we smashed them all unconscious they would have won the encounter. Can't you just hear them bragging about it? *You* must know how they go on, Phil, if anyone does.' Trevor was referring to Philip's job as a Social Security officer, and Philip recognized the strength of his friend's argument. He knew, all right. Hadn't he heard them often enough in the caller section at his area office—blowing their trumpets about their encounters with rival gangs. The more it took to beat them, and the harder they were hit, the greater their reflected glory.

'Yes, Trevor's right,' he told his neighbours reluctantly. 'We'd just be making heroes of them.'

'Well, what, then? Tell us what else we can do,' was the cry now on all their lips.

'Why don't we treat them like the weak-minded scum they are?' Philip said slowly. 'Like backward illiterates who need a well-deserved smack . . . Let's get them sandwiched between us and treat them like naughty babies . . . Put them over our knees and smack their bottoms soundly,' he finished with a gleam in his eye. A stunned silence followed, then a ripple of appreciative amusement rose and swelled to a yell of approval as the men each arrived at the same picture in his own mind.

'By golly, Phil. You've hit it!' One of them gave voice to the approbation of them all. 'That would really put them where they belong!'

'And after—after we've called the police to come and cart them away, we'll give the whole story to the local press. Can you imagine how that would grab 'em?' Excitement lifted George's voice to a falsetto squeak.

Satisfied now that the heat was gone from the situation and things could be safely left to go their own way, Trevor stepped down from the stool. Some of the suggestions being bandied about were getting a bit ribald, but better that by far than the lynching talk they'd been using earlier, he thought thankfully.

The meeting eventually broke up on a note of jocular determination. Philip went around the house emptying ashtrays and opening windows to clear the fug, his easy-going temperament somewhat restored by the camaraderie of the past couple of hours. He was happier now they had some plan of campaign, some organized arrangements for getting to grips with those mindless hooligans they'd been obliged to put up with for so long. All the hastily planned, scrambled attempts of the past were forgotten now as Philip mulled over their scheme. He felt certain it was going to work.

Crossing the hall on his way up to bed, he resolved to spend the following day getting the place back to some sort of order. The cut over his eye was healing well and his vision was clear enough to allow him to drive his car, so tomorrow he'd run round to the builder's merchant and see about getting the broken glass replaced for a start. Or maybe he wouldn't. His eyes narrowed in sudden contemplation of a new idea. Maybe it would be better if he bricked in the lower half of the glass panel. It was a big expanse of glass, Ann had often complained of it wasting heat, and if he got some of that ornamental stone to build a wall to about waist-high, he could leave the timber cross-piece to carry the letter-box and make a finished edge. There would still be sufficient light from the glass remaining. The more he thought about the idea, the more he liked it. A half-wall there would help reduce the damage from flying bricks, be safer for a toddler, and it would give them more privacy in the hall and stairs, besides having the added advantage of concealing any accumulation of mail from the chance passer-by, should he and Ann be away for a few days. That was something else Ann had complained of. He'd offered to fix up a mail-box, but she had said it would look ugly hanging in the middle of the glass. His new idea should solve all their problems. A jauntily whistled version of a popular song broke from him as he undressed, and a couple of adventurous trills as he hit a top note bore musical testimony to the upward swing of his spirits.

The consultant's sympathetic but resolute pronouncement

came as a slap in the face to Philip's rising hopes.

'I'm sorry, Mr. Butler. I did try to warn you,' he said, his eyes detailing the creamy white perfection of the long-stemmed roses dangling forgotten from Philip's grasp. He raised his eyes to meet Philip's agonized stare. 'Your wife is, um, very delicately, er, balanced at the moment. She must be transferred to a psychiatric hospital for a course of remedial treatment.'

Philip continued to stare at him, saying nothing.

'I wanted to keep her here, near the baby. In cases like this, Cæsarean births I mean, we like to establish contact between mother and child as soon as possible. I regret that will have to come second now.'

The silence following his speech stretched to the point where it became heavy, beating thickly against the walls of the small glassed-in office like a tangible thing. At last Philip dropped his blank stare from the other man's face and the movement of his eyes seemed to release them both from their state of suspension.

Philip cleared his throat and tried his voice experimentally. 'Is she . . .' he croaked, cleared his throat and tried again. 'Are you telling me my wife is . . . is . . .' He was unable to bring himself to say the word that would brand Ann as one of the lost souls whose minds are out of step with their bodies.

'Oh no. No, she's not insane.' The consultant said it for him and by his very ease of expression robbed the word of its nightmare qualities.

She has simply retreated a little into herself. It happens sometimes; the strain of the pregnancy, the conditions she has been forced to endure.' He shrugged, then spread his hands, indicating the impossibility of enumerating all the probable causes for Ann's condition.

'How long? . . . How bad is she?' Philip asked.

'It's difficult to say at this stage. She won't know you — or at least, she won't acknowledge you. But don't let that worry you too much, it's a common enough symptom. There are, er, other rather less pleasant manifestations of her disturbed condition, but overall I don't expect we shall have too much difficulty getting her back on her feet. We shall keep her here for the next eight days or so, then she will be transferred to the Green Lawns Nursing Home. You know it, do you? Just the other side of town?'

Philip nodded. He knew *of* it, as did most people who lived locally, but he had never expected to walk through its gates. The older man eyed him shrewdly, guessing some of the thoughts that were crowding his brain. 'There is nothing to be ashamed of, Mr Butler,' he said gently. 'Minds can become bruised just as easily as bodies.'

Philip managed an understanding smile. 'Yes. Yes, of course. And my wife has had a lot to endure.'

'Quite so.' A warm glance of approval accompanied the words. 'Now then. You can visit every day while she is here. Talk to her as you would under normal circumstances; see if you can get her to respond. Later I will arrange for you to see the doctor, who will be in charge of her case, and he will no doubt explain how best you can help.'

The silence began again. Before it could close in on them once more, Philip pushed his chair back with unnecessary vigour, something in him calling for action and the need to be part of the clatter and bustle going on outside these walls.

'I can see her now, can I?' he asked, his voice a shade overloud.

'Certainly. But remember, she may not make any response. If she should show any signs of distress, or even of interest for that matter, then please call the nurse.'

Philip entered the side-room Ann had been moved into with a freaky sensation of walking on tiptoe. He had no idea what to expect, was in fact distinctly nervous, and was vastly reassured to see Ann lying wide-eyed and silent, but otherwise looking much as she had when she first came into the hospital. 'Hello, darling,' he said. Ann's wide stare never faltered. 'Look, I've brought you some flowers.' He held the roses towards the bed. When Ann made no move to take them he looked helplessly around for somewhere to put them, and finally laid them across the table at the foot of the bed. He reached over and took her hand. The cool fingers lay across his palm as lifeless as a glove. He looked round the room seeking inspiration; what should he talk about? His eyes went back to that still form. What was she thinking? Was she thinking at all? He drew a deep breath and launched into speech.

'I . . . um . . . it's a lovely day out there,' he said, feeling more than a little foolish as Ann continued to stare silently at nothing in particular. 'Nice after all the rain . . . I put some new glass in the hall this morning,' he began, then kicked himself for a fool. She didn't want any reminder of the trouble they'd been having in her present state. Always supposing she could hear and understand him, he thought, then strangled that thought at birth. Of course she could understand him! She wasn't insane. She was going to be all right, and she would get better much quicker if he started by treating her like a normal human being.

Having made up his mind along those lines, Philip found it much easier to keep up his one-sided conversation. He told Ann all about the babies in the hospital nursery, making ridiculous jokes about their imaginary exploits in a vain attempt to wring a smile from her. He told her their little girl was a beauty. He promised her a new outfit once she came home and offered to take her down to London for a weekend of sight-seeing and shopping. No matter what he said, or how encouraging he made his suggestions, Ann never altered her silent gaze by as much as a flicker.

He was too upset and shaken to call in on Dawn and

Trevor when he got home from the hospital, and went straight indoors, preferring to keep his own company while he came to terms with this latest blow.

By mid-morning of the following day his weary head ached with his constant fretting at the same fruitless 'WHY!' of it all, and he was ready to pour out all his troubles when Dawn came across to ask how Ann was faring. She listened to the rush of words and was shocked, horrified and furious in turn.

'It's all the fault of those bloody morons,' she said through gritted teeth, tears of rage and sympathy putting a catch in her voice. 'Ann was always a sensitive little thing and it's all the worry over them that's brought her trouble on. How I wish I could just get my hands on them.'

'Well, given a bit of luck that's exactly what we aim to do. Didn't Trevor tell you what we've got planned?'

'Oh yes. He told me all right. And in the same breath he also told me he's putting our house up for sale,' Dawn said bitterly.

'Not still? Not if we manage to stop the raids? Oh, Dawn, no.'

'That's what *I* said. I said it would be stupid to move once the gang had been caught, but you know Trevor — ever the one for logical argument. He says there will be no way of knowing you've stopped them for good until you can look back on a couple of years free of trouble.'

'Oh hell! Well, look, don't let Ann even get a whiff of your plans, will you? Not until she's home and — and better again. She'd be dreadfully upset. Maybe, if you haven't found a buyer by then and we've got the raids stopped, maybe Trev will reconsider.'

'Huh! Maybe. But I wouldn't take any bets on it, Phil.'

They stared at each other in mutual commiseration.

Saturday was close and warm, the airless summer day giving way to a soft balmy breeze as the light began to pale from a painted evening sky. In the back garden of No. 1, the men from the houses on that side of the road stood about in twos and threes, or leaned against the dividing fence, carefully shielding their glowing cigarette-ends in the palms of their hands, in faithful imitation of that wartime observation of caution. There was a feeling of keen excitement charging the air between them. At the other end of the road, in the rear garden of No. 28, a similar group paced the neatly trimmed lawn and waited for some indication from their colleagues that their quarry had come into view. Philip was numbered among the men in this garden, as was George Turner, his next-door neighbour. They stood together, a serious pair a little apart from the more volatile knot of men gathered to hear the latest joke recounted by David Tomlinson, the acknowledged wag of their group.

Listening to David's low, rumbling whisper, waiting for the stifled laughter that would herald the punch-line, Philip wondered aloud how it came about that their group, all young men, could meet together without thought of doing damage to anyone's property, while the hooligans they waited for seemed hell-bent on inflicting damage and waste wherever they went.

'I dunno, Phil,' George said slowly in response to Philip's whispered remarks. 'Maybe they're jealous, maybe they're sick. Maybe they've had deprived childhoods. You know, like all the do-gooders would have us believe. Or maybe they haven't had enough good hidings,' he added darkly.

'Yeah, that's the more likely,' Philip concurred. 'There's too much of the kid-glove treatment these days.'

'What are you two doing, then? Putting the world to rights over here, are you?' The speaker was a middle-aged man, the oldest resident of the Grove, having moved into No. 20 following a second marriage.

'That's right, Harry. We were just defining the basic cause of hooliganism these days,' George informed him.

'Parents!' said Harry succinctly.

'Parents?'

' 'Sright. Parents. You must have seen them. *And* heard them. There's even some right here I could mention.'

'Go on,' Philip urged, giving the senior man his full attention.

'Well, it starts with the toddlers, doesn't it? You must have noticed. Little Johnny wants to climb up somebody's fence or whatever. Daddy says no. Little Johnny goes right ahead and does it anyway. And what does Daddy do? Nothing. He waits usually till little Johnny is ready to climb down. Now, it's my opinion that if you can't, or won't, make 'em do as they're told at that age, then there's not a cat in hell's chance of controlling them when they get into their teens.'

'You've got grown-up kids, have you?' George was aware, as were the rest of their neighbours, of the young adults who came and went, seeming to spend quite a length of time at Harry Knight's home, though he had never been sure whether they were friends or Harry's children from his first marriage. He seized this opportunity of satisfying his curiosity.

'Three. Two boys and a girl,' he was told. 'All of them decent, well-balanced kids who know their places.'

'So you are saying start the discipline while they are small?' Philip asked with genuine interest.

'I am. I am also saying a few smacked bottoms never came amiss either, never mind all this bullshit the modern psychos dish out. I mean, look at Mike Challoner's two lads.'

Philip and George turned to gaze in the direction Harry indicated with a jerk of his head. Mike, a big gangling chap, was standing, head down, listening to yet another of David Tomlinson's jokes. They concentrated their glance as if by doing so they would see his five-year old twins.

'Mischievous, he calls them.' Harry's voice dripped scorn. '*Mischievous*, when they put the cat in the washing-machine and switched it on. *Mischievous*, when they painted the youngster from next door bright green from head to toe. *Mischievous* again, would you believe, when they started a fire under their bed with a box of matches and an old newspaper. Mischievous isn't the word *I* would use for those two. You mark my words, they are vandals of the next generation and no mistake.'

Philip drew a deep breath and considered Harry carefully. Until this moment he had given no real thought to the ongoing responsibilities of being a parent. A baby to him had been simply that — a baby. Something small and sweet for Ann to pet and cuddle, his own involvement having always seemed somewhat shadowy. Now he saw it through different eyes. His child would one day emerge as a full-grown adult, and the type of adult she became would, according to Harry at least, owe a lot to his guidance. The idea was mind-blowing. Philip opened his mouth to protest this overwhelming responsibility and was immediately silenced by a hissing.

'Shh.' An electric whisper charged the group of men, checking the careless chatter that had been growing ever louder. They looked at each other in anticipation. Was this it?

The measured tread grew ever nearer. Heavy boots walking in step. They waited for the sounds of pursuit from their colleagues.

'It's only the police.' A gasp sounded in the small garden as thirteen men expelled their breath in unison.

'God. That's shot it,' George whispered to Philip. 'The gang will never show while the police are patrolling. You know how it was the last time.'

'Yes, and the minute they're recalled the trouble will start all over again,' Philip whispered back.

'It would be better for us if we're not caught waiting

around like this, either,' Harry advised. 'The sergeant was pretty adamant about us not taking the law into our own hands.'

'We'll wait a while, let the bobbies get out of the Grove, then we'd better call it a night,' a voice loaded with the disgust they were all feeling instructed.

'Yeah. This is one time we could have well done without the boys in blue,' said George, speaking with no fear of contradiction.

CHAPTER 5

Philip went back to work on Monday morning with all the reluctant depression that more frequently followed a care-free holiday break. Ann had shown no signs of improvement over the weekend. She was due to be transferred to Green Lawns Nursing Home later in the week. Their tiny daughter continued her battle for life without any marked change within her glass incubator, and the louts responsible for her precipitate entry into the world were still at liberty. The cheerless grey bricks of the Social Security building matched Philip's mood. Bleak, soul-destroying and cold, the impersonal shell housed the bustling offices that saw so many of life's all-time losers.

Crossing the antiquated entrance hall, with its white-tiled walls cracked and crazed with age, he ignored the door to the left that bore the word RECEPTION in large black letters across its eau-de-nil paintwork, and shouldered his way through the double swing-doors into the over-powering reek of disinfectant that waited for him on the other side. He would know that smell anywhere. Strong enough to stop the breath in the throat at first acquaintance, it gradually thinned to reveal the odour of unwashed bodies and urine-soaked clothing it was ineffectually

employed to cover. Following the warren of narrow corridors that intersected the old building, he crossed behind
the caller section, at this hour empty of importuning
claimants, and mounted the stairs leading to the large,
heavily staffed assessment section. His desk was at the far
end of the room. An accumulation of case-papers had
found their way on to its surface, spilling out of the in-
tray and across the Government Issue blotter in untidy
array.

Oh God. His spirits sinking even lower, Philip fixed his
eyes on the pile as he moved down the office. Was there
no end to this, this constant calculation of other people's
weekly allowances? The chorus of ' 'Morning, Philip'
from his colleagues passed unheard until a bright, welcoming voice interrupted his gloomy thoughts, and he
turned to answer the girl sitting behind a desk as thickly
covered as his own.

'I said, hello, Philip. How are you?' the girl repeated
with a smile. Helen Broadhurst had joined the service
only twelve months ago. She had come straight from college
with enough GCE.s at A-level to win her an immediate
place as an Executive Officer. Some of the old hands,
having been in the service since the days when it was called
the National Assistance Board, now affectionately referred
to by all and sundry as the Nab, resented her easy placing.
They had worked, and worked damned hard in their
opinions, for their slow promotions from Clerical Assistant
Third-Class through to a position and salary still below
that held by this untried girl. And they made sure she was
not allowed to forget it. The full, rather evocative figure,
and the attractive face framed by hair worn loose to the
waist, did nothing to temper their snide remarks. She
rode their animosity with seeming indifference, and only
to Philip did she ever reveal how deeply she felt the
wound of their words. The fact that she hated her job did
nothing to make her life any easier. She had applied

again and again for a transfer out of the department, but this was the branch currently most in need of qualified officers, and it seemed that it was here she must stay.

Philip had secured his promotion from Clerical Assistant to Clerical Officer by local board, and though this left him inferior in position and salary to Helen, he felt none of the resentment exhibited by his older colleagues. On the contrary, as his immediate superior who did her share of the work and took no advantage, the girl commanded both his sympathy and his respect. He acknowledged her greeting and did his best to summon an answering smile.

'Oh hello, Helen. I'm not bad—at least, I wasn't until I saw all this lot.' He waved a hand towards his cluttered desk. 'What's going on? We're not uprating again, are we?'

' 'Fraid so. It's the council tenants' rent increase. They're due to go up next month, remember?' Helen tossed back her long curly hair and picked up a bulging file. 'Can't keep the claimants waiting, Phil. They might suffer hardship,' she said on a note of sarcasm. She pulled a sour face as she leafed through the contents of the file. 'Oh hell! Six kids, two earning, one in care, and a lodger. It'll take me ages to work that one out.' She slapped the papers down in disgust. 'Oh, never mind them for ten minutes, let's hear about you. I gather you've been in the wars. Not to mention police custody,' she ended with a laugh.

'Rubbish! I only saw the sergeant once, I was out visiting Ann when he came back. Who told you, anyway? Your brother?' Philip asked, knowing Helen's brother was on the local police force.

'Stephen? Oh no. No, he seldom talks about his work, and he's been transferred now to the CID. So I don't suppose he'll be involved with the more bread-and-butter stuff. No, I heard it from E.J.'

'Oh, he does know I exist, then?' The question held a

touch of rancour. E. J. Hazeldine was the officer in charge of their department. Philip pushed the piles of case-papers to the edge of his desk and parked himself in the cleared space, prepared for a gossip.

He didn't feel like getting to grips with any problems but his own as yet, and Helen was ever a ready listener. By the time he'd brought her up to date with his affairs, his black mood had lifted considerably, and he applied himself to the task of working through his quota of case-papers. Helen rewarded his diligence with a dimpled smile.

And so the week continued, with a work-load so heavy that Philip had very little time to brood on his troubles. He had the stitches removed from his eye on Tuesday and Ann was moved out to Green Lawns Nursing Home on Wednesday afternoon, as planned. Philip had a long interview with Dr Richardson, her consultant psychiatrist, that evening. He emerged from the deluge of words the man had poured at him feeling little better informed than when it began. He gathered that Ann was by no means unique, that a great many women succumbed to the mental traumas of childbirth, and that time, that ever-constant panacea, was all that was needed to put things right in her case.

When his parents phoned from the pub they kept in Somerset, he was able to add very little to the information he had already given them. In response to his mother's anxious offer to come over for a few days to give him a hand, he assured her that he was coping very well and that he would rather she postponed her visit until either Ann or the baby, or both, were allowed home.

'How is the baby? Is she making progress?' His mother's voice was as clear over the miles as if she was standing at his elbow.

'She's fine,' he said. 'Looks just like you.' This was a lie. To Philip, in spite of the ounces she had gained in the last couple of days, his daughter still looked slightly less than human.

'Oh, the little lamb. I'm longing to see her. Oh, hang on a minute, love — don't put those light ales there, Sally,' Philip heard her call through to the barmaid. 'They're too near the strip-light, they'll get warm.' Philip had a mental picture of the long, brightly lit bar, and felt a stir of nostalgia for the beery, smoky atmosphere and the friendly companionship that went with it. If Ann wasn't home at the weekend, he'd take a walk up to the local and try a jar or two, he promised himself.

'Sorry about that, Phil.' His mother came back to the phone. 'You need to have eyes in the back of your head where staff are concerned. And I'll have to leave you now, son. Your dad's gone down to the cellar and there are people waiting to be served. Ring me tomorrow, will you?'

'Sure thing, Mum. Be good, both of you,' said Philip, fondly shaking his head as he replaced the receiver. His mother always took life on the run, she'd meet herself coming back one of these days.

The loud black and yellow FOR SALE sign outside No. 11 was the first thing Philip noticed as he turned his battered old Morris into Lynden Grove on his way home from the office on Friday evening. He'd been feeling particularly cheerful, with a week's hard work behind him, and a more optimistic report from Green Lawns still sounding in his ears — and now this! He stared at the sign resentfully, so preoccupied he almost missed the turn into his drive.

'Damn, damn, damn.' He thumped dejectedly on the steering-wheel with the edge of his clenched fist. He had been relying on Dawn's strength of character to override Trevor's decision to move out. Lynden Grove wouldn't be the same for Ann and himself without their friends over the way. And what effect their departure would have on

Ann he could only guess—but it wouldn't be good. He heaved a deep sigh of regret as he reached for the door handle. Oh well, he could hardly dictate what others should do, he thought dolefully, as he pushed the door wide and climbed out of the car.

Dawn must have been watching for his arrival, for he had hardly fitted his key into the front door when she arrived at his elbow. 'You've seen it, I expect?' she asked without preamble.

'Yeah,' Philip said heavily. 'I'm sorry, Dawn. I was sort of hoping you'd change Trevor's mind.'

'Ordinarily, yes. This time, no way. I've argued till I'm black in the face.' She lifted her shoulders expressively.

'Got anywhere lined up yet?'

'No—Oh hell, come on, Phil. Open the door, I'll scratch you a meal and make us both a cup of coffee, then we can cry on each other's shoulder.'

He pushed open the door and waited for Dawn to precede him into the hall. 'No need for you to bother with a meal, Dawn. I ate at work, but I'll take you up on the coffee.'

'Okay.' She led the way into the kitchen. 'I hate it, Phil. This running away, I'd much rather stay and face those thugs. It makes my blood boil when I think how we're letting them push us about.'

Philip felt exactly the same, but he resisted the urge to side with her against Trevor's decision. He could see she was so angry and upset that any interference would only result in a bitter quarrel between husband and wife. Swallowing his own disappointment, he said placatingly, 'I expect we will probably move out too; I mean, once the baby comes home I won't want her upset, any more than Trevor wants Mark and David disturbed by it all.'

Dawn looked at him keenly, then said with deliberation, 'No you won't. I know you, Philip. You'll stand and face them, like Trevor should if he had any guts. He just makes the boys an excuse.'

Feeling somehow responsible for Dawn's scathing attack on his friend, Philip did his best to mend matters, but was left with the uneasy feeling, when Dawn eventually went back to her home, that she was more than ready to make the issue an excuse to transfer her affections, should he so desire. Perhaps it's just as well they are moving, he thought guiltily as he changed his suit, ready to make his self-promised visit to the pub. He'd better watch his step, she was a bit of a firebrand, was old Dawn.

He passed a rather lonely couple of hours at the Bull, the nearest of the two council-estate hostelries, and left without regret as the landlord dipped the lights for closing time. He'd lost the art of drinking alone since he'd been married, and he missed Ann's company badly. Still, he'd be able to visit her tomorrow, and if today's report from the nursing home was half way correct she would be ready to talk to him.

All unsuspecting, he strode into the open gateway of his front drive and promptly measured his length. The air was driven from his lungs by the sledge-hammer force of his fall. Sprawled inelegantly on the ribbed concrete, whooping loudly for breath, he was dimly conscious of the jeers and laughter that preceded the drum of running footsteps. Pushing himself to sitting position, he began to swear even as the lights came on along the Grove and the doors of the neighbouring houses were opened to spill their occupants into their front gardens.

'Hey, Phil. What're you doing down there?' George Turner leaned over the wall and stared in disbelief at Philip sitting in the middle of his drive.

'Playing marbles.' Philip couldn't resist the sarcasm as he got to his feet and went to investigate the cause of his downfall. 'Bastards.' The tightly drawn wire was tied just below knee-height across his driveway. It was fastened in such a manner that had he driven into it in the car he would probably have demolished both his gate-posts.

George, unperturbed by Philip's crushing reply, joined him in the gateway. 'But it's only Friday,' he was saying stupidly as angry exclamations from along the Grove revealed further discoveries of damage.

Soon, every house was showing light as more of their neighbours belted themselves into dressing-gowns and ventured out to check on the state of their property.

'They've really got us taped, haven't they?' The errant schoolteacher's deserted wife stared woefully at the huge coping-stone which had once topped her gate-post and was now perched on the bonnet of her mini. 'I never leave the car out at weekends, so now they switch their nights.'

'They must have seen the police patrol last weekend,' said someone from the edge of the crowd.

'And this is their way of letting us know,' said Philip flatly.

'Well, what do we do now?' The question was posed by David Tomlinson. 'Do we all sell up and clear out—' he cast a quick glance in Trevor's direction— 'or do we keep watch every night until we catch the sods?' The discovery of his much-prized flowering cherry cut to a bare four-feet-high stump had damped his normal wit.

'We keep watch every night.' Philip's voice carried enough determination to convince them all. 'We'll draw up a rota and have four men, two at each end of the close, every night from now until this thing is settled.'

'I can't figure it out. How the hell do they keep abreast of our every move in this way? It's uncanny.' The remark produced a spate of agreement.

'It's almost as though they had our homes bugged,' George ventured to say.

'Now, don't let's get carried away. This may be the age of electronics, but this *is* England and they—'

'And they are going to get all that's coming when I get my hands on them,' Philip cut in grimly. And it was on

this note of determination that the gathering broke up.
But not before they had all agreed to start their nightly
vigil without further delay.

A purposeful tattoo sounding on his front door early the
following day sent Philip hurrying to answer its summons.
Brian Goss, his right leg still in plaster, was leaning
against the door-frame, a walking-stick clutched firmly in
his hand.

'Hey! Come in, Brian. Glad to see you getting about.'
Philip held the door wide as Brian manœuvred his way
over the step and into the hall.

'I've come to see you about those plans you have for
catching up with those bloody night-riders,' he said,
punctuating his words with gasps for breath as he heaved
the weighty plaster cast along.

'Sit down then, man. Before you fall down.' Having
steered him towards a stout upright chair, Philip eased
Brian on to its seat.

'I got a letter-box full of shit this morning.'

The bald statement caused Philip to stare. What on
earth did he mean? Had he been in receipt of some ob-
noxious mail?

Before he could ask, Brian said again: 'Shit! Human
shit. Dianne put her hand in the letter-box straight into
it — Christ, she was as sick as a dog.'

Philip felt himself gag in sympathy.

'Just give me ten minutes alone with one of those dirty,
stinking sods.' Brian clenched his fingers over the top of
his walking-stick as if anticipating that meeting.

'There's not much you can do at the moment, not with
that leg.'

'I could be one of the ones to keep watch.'

'Not really, Brian. I mean, once whoever's on duty
spots the first sign of trouble he's going to have to move
like greased lightning to get round as many of the rest of

us as possible without giving the game away and scaring them off. It will need most of us there to be sure of catching them all.'

Brian considered this information for a moment or two, then asked: 'How are you planning to pass the word along?'

'Well . . .' Philip shrugged helplessly. 'It'll be a case of nipping across the back gardens and knocking on doors. What else can we do?'

'I could rig up an alarm system, if you like. What's the use of learning a trade if you can't make use of it?'

'Hey, yes. I'd forgotten you are an electrician. How would you do it?'

'I'd need to give that some thought, but I'm sure I could lay a bell connection to each house, with a hand-switch for the blokes on watch. Then all they'd need to do to arouse the rest of you is press it.'

'Now that's just what we need. How soon could you manage it?'

'I'll get cracking right away.' Brian held out his hand for Philip to assist him to his feet. 'Give me a couple of hours, then come round, Phil, would you? Just in case I'm short of anything. Can't get up to the shops myself with this thing.' He tapped the plaster cast.

'Righto, Brian. I'll call on my way out to visit Ann,' Philip promised, opening doors to let his neighbour out. Things were looking up at last. Now they were getting properly organized, they should soon be able to come to grips with those scum.

True to his promise, he called at No. 4 on his way out and collected a short list of requirements from Brian.

'I've checked along the road, Phil, and there are only about half a dozen of us without front-door bells, so what I propose to do is link them all by a trailing wire passing across the front of each house. It'll be a bit untidy and a bit inconvenient for a time, but with a bit of luck it won't be for long. I'm going to connect them all up to a couple of batteries and they are among the things I want you to get, if you will.'

'You bet. Just say the word, old chum, and the world will be yours,' Philip promised grandly.

'I'd settle for a crack at those dirty swine, but since I'm a bit handicapped at present this will just have to be my contribution. Although,' he went on in mock seriousness, 'I suppose I could turn my talents towards building an electric chair.'

'And that's not such a bad idea,' said Philip as he took his leave.

His shopping duties discharged, he wound his way through the traffic on the one-way system and took the B road out of town. The nursing home was a good ten miles away by car and he experienced a burst of sympathy for anyone obliged to do their visiting by courtesy of the erratic public transport system.

As the sister had confidently predicted, Ann was beginning to show signs of regaining her interest in life. She wasn't yet up to holding any sort of conversation, but at least the awful blank stare was broken, and she responded to most of his deliberately cheerful small talk with a fairly intelligent air.

'Don't try her too far, not at first,' the psychiatrist had cautioned. 'Keep to generalities if you can. And watch her carefully when you mention the baby. If she shows signs of distress then drop the subject immediately.'

Philip found himself so inhibited by this instruction that he was unable to raise the subject of their daughter at all, and left the nursing home promising himself he would find some way to tackle it the next time he came.

Later that evening he and George Turner, working under Brian's instructions, went stealthily about rigging up their warning bell system.

'Better not make a parade of it,' George cautioned. 'You never know if they've got somebody keeping conk for them. And I would just hate to scare 'em away now.'

'Too true,' Philip agreed.

So they strolled as nonchalantly as they were able, up and down the front drives, paying out the lengths of bell-wire between them. Brian's progress as he called at each house to complete the link-up provoked a great deal of amusement between them.

'Oh God,' Philip spluttered, watching him make a Charlie Chaplin parade with his plaster cast and walking-stick as theatrical props. 'He only needs a moustache and he'd be the living image.'

The wiring completed, George and Philip retired indoors, their parts done for the day. The four men standing first watch had been given instructions regarding the use of the bell, and they took up their posts at ten o'clock prompt.

At 11.15 the system was given an impromptu trial run when Mike Challoner, who was in charge of the switch for his side of the Grove, gave it an involuntary squeeze. No hard feelings were felt by the men who hastily answered the summons, since they were all agreed that their being assembled so swiftly just went to prove the efficiency of their plan.

'I think we might as well jack it in for tonight anyway,' said Mike. 'The only signs of life we've seen have been the police patrol, and that bloody cat from No. 7 scratting up Trevor Austin's chrysanths.'

CHAPTER 6

The watch was mounted again on Sunday night, but all remained quiet. In truth, not one of them anticipated any further action until the following weekend, and in this mood of anti-climax were all for abandoning their former plans to keep a watch every night. It was only at Trevor's insistence that they went through the motions of drawing up a duty roster.

'We'll look a right lot of chumps if they catch us out again,' he pointed out. 'And I don't mind waiting out there for a month if that's what it's going to take.'

'Yeah, I s'pose you're right. Come on, then, let's get sorted out who does what.' Mike Challoner added his powers of persuasion in Trevor's support and the rest of them fell in with good grace.

Since they were all eager to be detailed for the key nights of Friday, Saturday or Sunday, there was a considerable amount of open-handed cheating with the dice they used to throw for their chance. So much so that by the time everyone was finally allocated a night for duty their temporary low spirits had become a thing of the past and they broke up to spend what was left of their Sunday night dreaming dreams of what they would do when they eventually came to grips with their tormentors.

Arriving at the Social Security offices on Monday morning, Philip was met in the entrance hall by a knot of men all jostling in the crowded space to get a look at a list pinned to the staff notice-board. As the swing-doors flapped together behind him, several heads bobbing on the edge of the group were turned enquiringly in his direction, only to turn immediately back towards the board once his face had been identified.

'You're on this, Phil,' one of his colleagues informed him with a jerk of his thumb at the board.

'What's that, Tom? Somebody giving away fivers?' he grinned as he edged his way into the midst of the group.

'Some hopes! It's strike duty. The steel workers this time.'

Philip elbowed his way through the crush to read the list of those personnel required to report at the emergency payment centres being set up around the foundries. His own name was bracketed together with that of Helen Broadhurst, Clive Davies, and Jake Titterton and appeared against the Nestra Ironworks, a small foundry situated about fifteen miles away. Some of the staff, he noted, were being sent to lodging-out areas, which meant a chance of extra money by way of subsistence and travel payments. He could have used a bit extra himself just now, what with all the things they would need for the baby. Still, he didn't really want to be posted too far from home at the moment, he thought in immediate contradiction, not with the way things were. And he supposed the four of them detailed for Nestra would take it in turns to use their cars, so he'd gain a bit by way of a petrol allowance. At least it would make a change from rent increase cases, he told himself philosophically. His listed companions, however, did not all share his easy acceptance of this change in their daily routine.

Clive Davies, in his late fifties and never over-industrious, complained bitterly about his arbitrary conscription. 'It's not bloody fair,' he fumed at Helen. 'We've got all this work on here and we're being sent to spoon-feed a load of sodding strikers who never ought to be getting paid anyway, in my opinion. They've got jobs to go to, so let 'em go to 'em — or starve.'

Helen shrugged and said defensively, 'I don't make the rules, Clive. I'm the same as you, I just do as I'm told.'

'Yes, and get precious little thanks for it.' Clive was not

to be placated. 'Who is it gets all the brickbats? — Tell me that! And who is it Joe Public's so quick to condemn? Bloody civil servants, that's who. Can't do right for doing wrong with most folk, but they don't see this side of it, do they?'

'Never mind, Clive,' Jake Titterton soothed. 'Look at all the overtime you'll draw.'

'Overtime! Don't give me bloody overtime. Not when we're paying those sods more in Supplementary than I earn in a month.'

Philip listened without comment. He had a certain sympathy with Clive's angry remarks. After all, there was more than a gleam of truth in all he was saying. But even so, it was no use sounding off at Helen. Like she said, she was in the same boat as the rest of them.

It took most of the morning for them to clear their current cases for payment, and they were obliged to delay their departure for the strike centre until after the lunch-break. 'No point in looking too eager,' Helen counselled drily. 'Else they'll think we're enjoying ourselves.'

Between visiting the hospital to check on the baby, motoring out to visit Ann, and travelling backwards and forwards to the strike centre, Philip found his time fully occupied. He'd drawn Wednesday as his night to keep watch for the vandals, and he turned out at ten o'clock as arranged, feeling too tired to work up a great deal of enthusiasm. He'd been paired with Barry Simpson from No. 14, and they met in the rear garden of Barry's home, crossing over the intervening back gardens to arrive at the end of the row where they were to keep watch until midnight.

'Don't think we'll be in any bother tonight, Phil. Do you?' Barry asked in a whisper.

'Shouldn't imagine so. Hope not, anyway, I'm too bloody knackered to start chasing anybody tonight.' He yawned hugely and groped around in the flower tub at the rear of

No. 28, where he expected to find the bell switch. Having located it, he passed it to Barry, saying: 'Hang on to that, my old son, just in case, though. And don't press it, for God's sake. Not accidentally. I couldn't stand an inquisition right now.'

They waited in silence for some time, Philip propped against the wall of the house and staring up into the night sky, while Barry squinted round the corner, faithfully keeping watch along the length of the Grove for any signs of activity.

'Bit of a devil, old Trevor selling up, isn't it?' he asked over his shoulder.

'Yup! Wish he wasn't, but still . . .'

'June tells me she saw some people looking round their place this afternoon. She was wondering if Dawn would tell them about all this.' He held the bell switch aloft in explanation.

'Shouldn't think so.' Pushing himself upright from his slumped position against the house wall, Philip crossed the lawn to crouch behind a lilac bush that would hide him from the road while allowing him a good view along its length. 'She'd be a bloody fool if she did,' he whispered across to Barry as his thoughts returned to their discussion.

'Bit naughty, though, if she doesn't.'

'Would you?' Philip demanded sharply, forgetting the need for caution.

'Well—well, no . . . P'raps not.'

'There you are, then. In any case we'll have it all sorted out and over by the time anybody wants to move in.'

'I hope you're right. I'm getting so's I hate living here, yet I wouldn't have the nerve to sell out . . . seems a bit underhand and, well—defeatist to me. Although I quite see Trevor's point about it being best for the children,' he added hastily, sensing Philip's impatience with his remarks.

'We can all say what we would and what we wouldn't do,' came the censorious reply, 'and we'd all be best minding our own business.'

After that, the two men continued their vigil in silence. Barry's criticism of Trevor had rankled oddly with Philip, destroying whatever cameraderie they might have shared. Probably because he's only saying what I'm trying not to think, he told himself honestly in an attempt to analyze his feelings. But the die had been cast, and neither he nor Barry enjoyed their stint on watch very much.

By Friday the improvement in Ann's condition was such that Philip was encouraged to broach the subject of their baby. Watching his wife's smiling face with care, he asked: 'What about giving our daughter a name then, Mrs Butler? Don't you feel it's about time?'

'Name?' A puzzled frown replaced the smile and a shutter dropped somewhere behind the penny-brown eyes.

'That's right, darling. A name. Betty? Josie? Margaret? Rose? Come on now, tell me which you fancy.' Perfectly aware of her preference, Philip played out the game. Ann had decided the minute she knew she was pregnant on Matthew Charles for a boy, and Melanie Jane for a girl. He was pinning so many hopes on her remembering that. Besides, he thought ruefully, it was a little late to change things now, since the child had been baptized and the birth registered in the names Ann had chosen.

'Not Rose,' said Ann now, and Philip held his breath, willing her to say Melanie in the sweet way she had that made the name sound so pretty. 'No. Not Rose,' came again her only response.

'Don't worry, don't worry,' was the nursing sister's sturdy advice to him when he consulted her later. 'She's come a long way in a very short while. Just give it a little longer. She'll be all right.'

He drove home slowly, reluctant to face the empty

house and anxious, despite the sister's assurance, over Ann's seeming inability to fit herself into the maternal role. She had been so desperately eager to have a child, so ecstatic when they knew the baby was on its way. It seemed impossible that all those feelings could have been so completely wiped out. And all because of some worthless scum whose greatest pleasure in life appeared to be terrorizing the hapless inhabitants of Lynden Grove.

Mindful of the previous Friday night's débâcle, he garaged the car, locked the garage door and went back along the short driveway to secure the double gates. He paused in the gateway to cast a quick glance up and down the road. Everything looked perfectly innocent. He checked his watch, 8.49. Hmm, too early yet for any trouble. He gave a wave to Dawn, peering out of her front window, and called a meaningful good-evening to George Turner across their boundary wall. George would be one of the men keeping watch later on, and Philip interpreted his steepled fingers and piously raised eyes to be a prayer for a fruitful sojourn. He was obliged to chuckle at George's expression, in spite of the serious purpose behind the pantomime.

Having cut himself a doorstep of bread and dripping, Philip made a pot of tea and carried this late-tea-cum-supper through into the lounge, where he switched on the television and settled in front of it. Twenty minutes later he became aware that the programme had changed from its original travelogue to a comedy sketch without him being conscious that it had happened. Placing the tray on the floor, he rose and switched off the set, then found himself standing aimlessly in front of the blank screen. It was now 9.35, too soon for the men detailed for tonight's watch to have left their homes yet. Philip rocked on his heels, trying to decide whether to make his way over the gardens and wait for them there, or to go openly round to George's and ask to be included in tonight's watching brief. His mind made up, he took the stairs two at a time, on his way to change into his track-suit and sneakers. He'd long decided it was no use attempting to come to grips with that mob in a business suit and slip-ons. Then he let himself quietly out of the back door and crossed the garden to George's, where he was admitted through the french window as though he had been expected, which indeed proved to be the case.

'Thought you'd have to come sticking your oar in.' George's welcoming grin belied the disparity of his words. ' 'Smatter of fact, I'm expecting half the men in the Grove to be out there tonight — wives an' all, I shouldn't wonder. I know I wouldn't miss it for all the tea in China.'

Philip acknowledged this possibility and said, half in apology: 'It's not that I'm trying to steal your thunder, George. But I was climbing the walls waiting for it all to begin. I'd have gone really loopy if I'd had to sit still any longer. I reckon tonight is going to be *the* night, don't you?'

'By God, I hope so. I'm just geared up ready to do some-body a bit of no good.'

'Now just you watch what you're on with. I don't want you hurt,' his wife admonished, a worried frown drawing her brows together.

'Don't fret, Sue. Don't fret. I've told you, I'm going to tear their arms off and beat them to death with the soggy end,' George leered in exaggerated relish.

'Oh, get off with you, and don't be so daft,' said Sue, laughing now, well used after five years of marriage to her husband's brand of humour.

'Come on then, Phil. To battle.' George stepped out of the french door and slid it noiselessly across behind Philip. 'We'll be all right, Sue. Don't worry,' he whispered through the narrowing gap before the door snicked home.

Sue pulled her face in an affectionate grimace before pursing her lips in a silent kiss.

As George had predicted, he and Philip were joined by most of the men from their side of the road. They drifted into the garden in ones and twos, each with a muttered excuse for his presence. When the head count reached double figures George nudged Philip and whispered, 'Wonder if it's the same down the other side?'

'I should think so,' Philip whispered back. 'We're not going to need any alarm bells if those buggers turn up tonight.'

Time crept by on leaden feet. The men jostled silently for places that would give them a commanding view of the road, each of them hoping to be the first to spot their adversaries. As the luminous fingers of George's watch turned to 10.35 the first steady crunch of footsteps had them all sucking in their breath and flattening themselves back into concealment against the house walls. Hearts raced and stomachs turned somersaults in eager antici-pation, until a group of elderly gents, bound thirstily for the last half-hour at the Bull after their exertions in the indoor skittles match someone belatedly recalled seeing advertised at the church hall passed into their sight.

'Sod it! Sod it! Sod it!' The explosive whisper coming anonymously in the darkness released all their feelings, and they grinned sheepishly to themselves as they slowly relaxed.

'Too much of that and I'll need clean underpants,' said George succinctly. He tugged open the front of his jacket to form a protective screen into which he dipped his head to light a cigarette and re-emerge seconds later strength-ened by a cloud of tobacco smoke.

At 10.52 it started to rain. Beginning with a spasmodic drizzle, it settled to a true British downpour. As one man they hunched their shoulders and plastered themselves along the house wall, seeking what protection they could from the overhanging eaves. Nobody wanted to be the first to cry off, in fact nobody was in any real hurry to abandon his station, each of them feeling so sure this was the night that would see an end to the torment they had been obliged to endure.

At 11.15, soaked to their skins and totally dispirited, they squelched their way out into the road and plodded up their respective drives to drip on to their front-door mats before disappearing indoors. Only seconds after the last door had closed a similar group, emerging from the opposite end of the road splashed along the far pavement to disband as their neighbours had done.

And Friday night went gurgling down the drain.

Even the most optimistic among them didn't anticipate that their quarry would come within striking distance on Saturday. Not with the regular police patrol showing themselves to be very much on the alert. Trevor and Philip had met and held council during the day, both of them being agreed on the futility of maintaining the nightly watch until the following weekend.

'Like somebody mentioned before, it's uncanny the way they seem to know when it's safe for them to get up to their devilry,' Trevor observed.

'Oh, I don't know, Trev: I mean, you could hardly miss two great bobbies parading up and down, could you?'

'No, but how do they get to know so soon — soon enough to switch their night last week, for instance?'

Philip shrugged. 'Took a chance, I suppose. We haven't exactly made it difficult for them till we took this last stand, you must admit.'

'S'pose not, but still . . . And how does it come about they can sneak upon us the way they do wearing those sodding great boots? It makes me wonder sometimes if they haven't got supernatural powers. Stupid, I know, but I don't like it. It worries me.'

'Now don't start getting any spooky ideas, we've got enough on our plates without that. Anyway, I hear it's not going to be your worry for much longer — you've had people looking round, haven't you?' There was no note of censure in Philip's voice, just a wealth of genuine regret.

'I'll still be worried, Phil. I shan't just pack up and go without any thought for the rest of you, don't think that. It's simply that I'm not prepared to take any more. And as luck would have it, I can just about afford the move,' he ended honestly.

Philip punched him affectionately on the upper arm. 'I know, Trev. I'm not sitting in judgement. I hope you get your asking price. And it won't hurt any if we manage to get rid of those bastards in the meantime, will it?'

But even Philip was unprepared for the gratification of his hopes quite so soon. He was vulnerably naked, having decided upon taking a bath before he turned in, when the doorbell shrilled its alarm. 'Damn,' he muttered in annoyance. Who could be at the door at this time of night? He snatched up his dressing-gown with one hand and his discarded watch with the other. Ten minutes to midnight, what an hour to come calling. Even then the persistent, strident call did not register in the manner it was intended. Not until he was halfway down the stairs, knotting the dressing-gown cord about his waist as he went did the real purpose behind the continuous ringing cause his feet to freeze on the stair.

Christ! This was it. His blood began to race, a tingling rush of pins and needles as he turned about and galloped back up the stairs, almost missing his step as he bolted across the landing and into the bedroom. With fingers suddenly useless and clumsy, he threw off the tenaciously clinging dressing-gown and grabbed for his track-suit. His shoes, his shoes, where the hell were his shoes? Breathing fast, as though he'd already been running, he yanked open wardrobe doors, flinging Ann's footwear in all directions as he hunted for his sneakers. Hell's bells, if he didn't get a move on the whole shooting match would be

over and he'd have missed all the fun. Tossing aside the
frilled hangings, he finally located his sneakers under the
bed and rammed his bare feet into them. Then he was
off. Leaping down the stairs and out through the back
door, he blundered at breakneck pace across the back
gardens, to arrive gasping and eager at the rear of No. 28.

'Shhh!'

'Be quiet.'

'Belt up.' Angry exclamations were hissed at him from
the men already concealed in and around the garden. In
spite of his fear that he'd arrive too late to take any part in
the exercise, Philip discovered it had taken no more than
three minutes for him to get there. And he was by no
means the last, since a furtive crunching and scuffling in
his wake disclosed still more arrivals.

'Where are they? What's going on?' he hissed at the
nearest shadowy figure.

'They've just turned into the far end of the road. They
came over the fields,' came the reply.

'Well, what are we waiting for? Let's get up and at
'em.'

'Hang on, you bloody fool. If you rush in too soon you
could blow the whole shoot.'

'Has the alarm been sounded across the road?' someone
fretted impatiently.

'How the hell do we know?' Suppressed excitement
brought a sharp reply. 'We're here, aren't we? — and
that's all that matters. Just give 'em time to reach the
half-way mark, then we'll grab 'em.'

Philip stole across the garden, making for his previous
vantage-point behind the lilac bush. He slid into its leafy
concealment and almost fell over the two men already
crouching there.

'That you, Phil?' It was George Turner.

'Yeah, can you see them yet?'

'I can see them all right. Down by the gateway of that

second pair of semis. Get ready, they're moving this way now.'

Word ran round the gathering, and men rose from behind dustbins, coal bunkers, and shrubs; fists clenched, muscles taut, up on their toes and steaming for action. One long suspended moment and then:

'Yaaah!' The rallying cry came from the far end of the Grove and acted upon them like a starting pistol. Yelling mindlessly in reply, they poured round the side of the house and spilled out into the road to form an impenetrable human barrier.

CHAPTER 7

Their strategy proved excellent. The gang, taken completely by surprise, were trapped between the two pincers formed by the advancing men. Hideously inhuman in their grotesque vampire-adorned balaclavas, they scattered across the road, chasing backwards and forwards like demented squirrels as they sought to make their escape. A couple of them launched themselves in a mad scramble over George's front garden wall, hoping to gain access to the fields lying at the rear of the houses, but as soon as their ploy was spotted men moved across to yank them back into the group of their fellows being herded towards the pool of light cast by the central street lamp.

Seeing all avenues of escape closed to them, one youth, taller and seemingly older than the rest, began urging his companions to make a fight of it.

'Boot 'em! Boot 'em!' he screeched, suiting his actions to his words, and lashing out with his steel-capped feet in the direction of unprotected shins. 'Clog the bastards down. Go for their nuts.'

Eyes glinted savagely through the winged face-masks,

and spittle-rimmed caverns yawned red and curiously evil as mouths worked to spill out vile invectives and draw in gulps of air.

Philip found himself being forced into retreat as the viciously punishing feet lashed again and again in the direction of his groin. Blast Trevor and his pacifist ideas, he thought as he dodged yet another wild kick, we're going to lose them if this goes on. He tried once more to close on his opponent, but was obliged to jump back beyond the range of that booted foot. If only they'd brought something to lay about them with, as originally planned, they'd have had this settled in no time.

Preoccupied with his attempts to come to grips with the youth, who was now beginning to flaunt his mastery of the situation, Philip failed to hear the grunts and groans going on all about him. But a particularly high-pitched yell as a youth immediately to the left of his antagonist was brought to the ground gave him a sudden advantage. His attention temporarily diverted, the youth's flailing leg lost its previous accuracy and Philip side-stepped its swing before closing in swiftly to hook the other leg from beneath his assailant, who crashed backwards into the mêlée, bringing down another of his companions as he fell. Taking no chance of losing this advantage, Philip flung himself on top of the youth and grabbed for his throat. A wild exultation surged through him, the yielding flesh beneath his fingers triggering an unconquerable urge to punish and go on punishing until he had worked out all those weeks and months of suppressed and impotent rage. He was blind and deaf now to all but the wild beating of his own heart and the mad, joyous thrill of revenge.

'Philip! Philip, for Christ's sake!' He became aware of hands pulling him relentlessly away from the choking figure sprawled beneath him. The red cloud swamping his vision steadied and cleared as the vibrant music clamouring in his ears died away to a whisper.

'Eh?' he looked round at Trevor and Barry who held him in a restraining grip between them, looking alarmed.

'You might have killed him, you fool.' Barry was shaking in his anxiety.

Philip looked down to his feet where a crumpled form gasped and choked — one hand pushed under the long balaclava tenderly massaging the throat. He shook the restraining hands from his arms and straightened up. A silence had fallen on men and youths alike, caught up as they were in the dreadful primeval combat that had taken place in their midst. With Philip's release the spell was broken, but its sobering influence kept the helmeted gang passive captives.

Philip reached down and yanked the still choking youth to his feet.

'Steady, Phil.' Trevor's hand shot out to grip Philip's shoulder. 'Remember what we said.'

Philip stared at him blankly for a moment, then he grinned, all temper forgotten. 'Well now, Trev: shall you spank this bad boy, or shall I?' he asked.

The youth tried in vain to pull clear of Philip's bruising fingers. 'Gerroff, yer bastard,' he coughed out, a sudden premonition of impending ridicule giving him back his voice.

'Not yet, sonny. Not yet,' Philip said in a deliberately teasing tone, and he reached out to pull the concealing balaclava off the youth's head.

A brick-red face topped by a shaven bullet-shaped head that sported one earring pirate-style from beneath a fleshy left ear, was exposed to view. The eyebrows were black and well defined, the eyes beneath them slitted in anger, and the mouth, masked in part by a straggling wispy beard, drawn back in a snarl of pure animal rage.

'Anybody know this revolting-looking microbe?' Philip asked pleasantly, looking around the ring of faces.

'Wouldn't own to it, even if I did,' George called,

obligingly playing up to him.

'No, he's not a pretty sight.' Someone else caught the new drift and chipped in.

'Hmm, shall I use a slipper, do you think, or shall I drop his pretty blue knickers and slap his little botty with my hand?' Philip was clowning in over-reaction to his former loss of control.

'Get stuffed, you prat.' The youth lunged desperately, trying to break Philip's grip.

'Dear, dear. Such language! I shall have to wash your mouth out next, I can see that.' Some of the watching men shuffled uneasily, finding they didn't like this approach any better than the other extreme.

'Get on with it, Phil: give him a clout if you must, then let's get them all lined up for the police,' urged one of them.

With a swift thrust to the back of the youth's head, Philip tipped him off balance and held him across his partly raised knee. Raising his hand, he brought it down smartly with all the power of his shoulder behind it, and soundly belaboured the youth's behind.

The foul-mouthed abuse was swiftly replaced by yells of protest that in turn gave way to the flooding tears of abject embarrassment. Pushing the youth away in sudden disgust, Philip looked along the row of knitted helmets. 'Now then, how many more of you would like a dose of the same?' he asked quietly.

Glittering eyes stared back at him, emphasized by the pattern of black bat-wings. No one answered.

'Get those helmets off them.' Philip's voice dripped scorn. 'Let's see what abominations they're hiding.'

A brief scuffle ensued as the youths fought to keep their heads and their identities shrouded. But the superior strength and numbers of the Lynden Grove neighbours quickly quelled the futile outburst and left them gazing for the first time on the faces of their enemies. There were nine of them. All appeared to be somewhere between the ages of seventeen and twenty, and with one exception they were white. Most of them wore their hair cropped, one or two sported embryo beards, and a few had splashes of vivid colour dyed in haphazard fashion over their heads. There was a definite similarity in all their faces whether bearded or not, a certain aggressive cast to the features that made the shape of eyes and mouths almost identical. Even the tall black youth faded into the overall pattern, his inky-black skin securing no privilege of individuality among this group of look-alike faces.

'Well I'll be blowed,' one of the men was driven to exclaim after the first silent perusal. 'This one's a girl . . . Least, I *think* it's a girl.' His hand reached towards the chin and turned the face so that the full light from the street lamp lit its features.

The girl dropped her head all of a sudden and butted her captor unerringly across the bridge of his nose. There was a crack, audible to them all, before the blood spurted from his nostrils.

'Why, you vicious little—'

'Christine!' Shock, outrage, disbelief and hurt fought for a place in that one spoken name, bringing all heads round to stare at Harry Knight. His cry was followed by an incredibly loud brand of silence which held them all in its echoing span.

A positive chorus of questions sent the silence crashing as Harry stepped closer to stare at the defiant girl.

'Do you know her?'

'Who is she?'

'Know her, Harry?'

'Hey! What d'you know? Harry knows one of them.'

Harry made no attempt to answer the spate. His gaze was fixed on the girl, and only she, staring back at him, her upper lip lifted in a curl of contempt, saw the world die in his eyes.

'Christine.' This time the name was a croak. 'Why . . . ?'

'Be*cause*. That's why.'

'In the name of God,' he whispered.

'No! In the name of truth,' the girl blazed at him. 'All
this Mr Wonderful crap . . . you make me sick. Think
you've got it made, don't you? Think you can play around
with your bit of skirt, set up house with it, spend all your
time with it — ALL your time!' A derisive snort accompanied
the word, but the girl hadn't yet finished. 'You dote on it,
don't you? Lick its boots, and keep your *real* wife and kids
sweet into the bargain. Well, I'll tell you something now,
you randy old goat . . . You can stuff it up as often —' The
rest of her words were knocked reeling by the slap Harry
delivered to the side of her face.

The listening men shuffled their feet in some embarrassment as it came home to them that this foul-mouthed,
destructive little hell-cat was the daughter Harry had so
often held up to them as a shining example of well-adjusted
youth.

'All right, everybody. Get these creatures up by that
wall. I'll ring for the law.' Trevor placed a compassionate
hand on Harry's bowed shoulder. 'Do you . . . er . . .
about . . .' his fluttering gesture towards the girl asked the
question he was reluctant to voice.

'No, Trevor.' Harry straightened his spine. 'No, let her
take her chances with the rest of them.'

'Fair enough, Harry. If that's what you want, but I'm
sure none of us would . . .' Trevor let his sentence go unfinished as Harry shook his head. Turning about, Trevor
strode briskly away from the group and up his own front
drive, intent now on getting to the telephone that would
summon aid from the police and see this business settled
as swiftly as possible.

There were a few voluble protests from the gang of
youths as the men herded them towards the garden wall
of No. 16, but they seemed somewhat subdued now and

no further blows were exchanged. With the wall at their backs it made the task of containing them so much the easier. Harry Knight's daughter took up her position in the centre of them, her defiant stand proclaiming to the observer that she was indeed part and parcel of this band of marauders. The men ranged themselves round, some of them beginning to feel just a little foolish now that all the excitement of the chase and capture were past. But not Philip. He felt neither foolish nor forgiving — wasn't it his wife and child who were suffering because of these creatures? That thought alone fired his determination to see their tormentors justly punished. Roughly jostling a straying figure back into the knot of bodies, he felt with surprise a yielding softness under his touch. He stepped closer and peered at the skin lying soft and smooth along the sharp jawline.

'Oh, Lord,' he groaned in exaggerated dismay. 'There's another Joan of Arc here.'

'Well, let's just hope she's not as eager to be martyred,' someone said drily.

'Shouldn't think it likely,' said Philip, eyeing the girl with obvious distaste. 'Martyrdom takes courage, I'm told, which is something this scum have never heard about. All these are fit for is the cowardly destruction of other people's lives and property under the protective cover of darkness and those infantile hoods.'

'Aw, belt up, why don't yah?' The youth Philip had treated to a spanking regained enough of his former bluster to take up his role of gang leader. 'Who d'yah think you are anyway — General bloody Custer?'

Philip's corn-blond hair had attracted this type of comment before and he had his answer ready. 'And what if I do?' he asked with slow emphasis. 'You are no Sitting Bull, not by a long chalk, so just button your lip — before I decide to smack your bottom again.'

'You big-headed swine, you're gobby enough with your

mates around aren't you? But don't think you'll get away with this 'cos you won't. I'll get even with you, you shit-pot, wait and see if I don't.' The youth was almost sobbing with suppressed rage and two of Philip's neighbours had a difficult job to restrain him as he made a desperate lunge in Philip's direction.

'Philip, really—' Trevor re-appeared at his friend's elbow— 'hasn't this gone far enough? The police are on their way, should be here any second, so why don't you just cool it?'

Philip made the shorter man subject to a long stare of appraisal before he lifted his shoulders in a dismissive shrug. 'Suits me,' he said as he turned away.

True to Trevor's prediction, the police arrived within minutes. As the first of the two panda cars turned into Lynden Grove, a fresh scuffle broke out among the group of youths. 'Make a break for it, you looneys. Don't just stand there.'

'Come on, you clods, give it to 'em.' Their self-appointed leader took up the cry and urged them along, setting the example by striking out with fists and elbows as weapons as he began making a passage for himself through the imprisoning cordon of men.

'Stop him!'

'Hold them together.'

'Give 'em what for—ummph!' George's breath was ex-pelled with a gasp as he caught one of the flailing fists in the stomach. Navy-clad figures moved to his aid and the assault shifted back to the verbal as a few judiciously aimed blows fell among the leather-clad group.

'What's going on here? Let's have some order.' The police constable's authoritative bellow brought silence. 'Now then, who's going to give me the spiel?' His glance travelled enquiringly from one group to the other. The silence stretched out between them. Then, as if at a signal, they all began talking at once, explaining, accusing, condemnations, excuses and denials making a mad cacophony beating the ears with unintelligible sound.

The constable gave it a few minutes before he pointed his finger directly at George. 'You there. Care to step over here?' George strode importantly forward to accompany the policeman as he withdrew a few paces away from the din. 'Now then!' The two words were an invitation to speak and George plunged into an explanation of the evening's events.

'Did you actually *see* these—er people, causing any damage?' was the first question put to him as his voice tailed away.

'*See* them! We didn't need to *see* them, we've been living with the results of their vicious little attentions for God knows how long.'

'So no one, in fact, actually witnessed these things being done?'

'No, man, I keep telling you. We don't *need* to *see*, we *know* they're being done—and we know equally well who they're being done by.' George was rapidly running out of patience. Why weren't the police getting those scum rounded up and put behind bars where they belonged? Why stand here like idiots asking questions of him?

'You can prove that, sir, can you?'

'Eh?' George was so incensed by the constable's apparent neglect of his duty he had lost track of the conversation.

'Proof! I was asking can you give me any proof?'

'Of course I can give you proof. Ask Trevor Austin, ask that bloke there, with his nose bleeding. Ask Philip Butler, ask any of them, they can all tell you about it.'

'But I'm asking you; what proof do you have that those people there are the ones responsible for all the damage you complain of?'

'Christ Almighty, Officer! They're there, aren't they? What the hell more do you need!' The outraged demand carried clearly to the now intermingled bunch of interested spectators. Philip peered about him and finally located Trevor's puzzled gaze, his lack of inches having caused him to become swamped by the jostling shoulders about him. The message in Philip's grey eyes was quite clear. It demanded action from the smaller man, summoned him to support the efforts their friend George was making. Trevor responded, and pushed his way through the crush to join Philip, then the two of them approached George and the constable.

'If you'll check back with your base, Constable, you'll find this isn't the first time we have asked for police help to deal with these villains,' Trevor informed him. 'One of your sergeants, a Sergeant Parker, came out only a week or two past when my neighbour here—' he laid his hand on Philip's shoulder and drew him a little further forward— 'when he had his face laid open by a brick one of them threw at him. You can see the scar for yourself, the stitches only came out a few days ago.'

'And you claim that it was the same group of people responsible for that incident?' the constable asked, paying no particular attention to the livid scar over Philip's right eye and seeming more concerned with making a study of Trevor's earnest expression.

'There can be no doubt of it, Constable. These—these people have been systematically destroying our homes and our peace of mind for the past eight or nine months.'

Something of Trevor's conviction conveyed itself to the listening officer, and he pursed his lips thoughtfully before nodding his head in a barely perceptible motion which none the less signalled his apparent willingness to act on behalf of the householders. 'Radio for another car, Ewan,' he called to the policeman who had remained seated behind the wheel of the second panda car. The staccato crackle of static confirmed his request had been heard and acted upon.

'Are you arresting them?' Harry's troubled face appeared at George's shoulder.

'No, I wouldn't say that, not at the moment. We're just going to run them down to the station and take a few statements, like.'

'Then . . . could I come along . . . I . . . she . . . The girl there, that one . . .' his voice fell to a whisper. 'She's my daughter.'

As Harry pointed towards her the girl looked directly at him and caught the unmistakable gesture. 'Don't come doing me any favours, you bastard,' she yelled across the gap between them, already backing away as though pursued by an enemy. 'I can do without you and your bloody marvellous understanding—patronizing git.'

Harry let his arm drop.

'Perhaps you'd better come along, sir. We might be needing your statement anyway.' The constable sensed something of the older man's bewildered misery and deliberately softened his voice.

'Won't you be needing us all?' George demanded, eager to have his say and anxious that justice be made to prevail.

'Shouldn't think so, not tonight. Just give your names and addresses to the PC over there and we'll contact you if necessary.' The words were crisp and emphatic, leaving no room for further discussion. George, Philip and Trevor went obediently to join the group forming about the indicated constable as a third panda car pulled up behind its stable companions and the job of shepherding the nine belligerent youngsters into the back seats of the three vehicles began.

CHAPTER 8

Harry rode to the police station in the company of Constable 623 and three distinctly subdued hooligans. Separated from their companions, they seemed to shrink in stature, losing their identity until even their way-out hair-styles paled into the commonplace and Harry became distinctly aware of their mounting apprehension.

Nobody said much as the car sped in and out of the night-quiet suburbs, until they neared the town and the police station; then one of the youths, trying to throw off the restraint he'd been under, began to bawl a filthily worded version of an old-fashioned ballad. But the constable was quick to check his outburst with a few sharp words.

'I can sing if I want, can't I? Still a free country, ain't it?' The youth slumped further down in the back seat and began to tap out a drum rhythm on the back of Harry's seat.

'Leave that out!' Without taking his eyes off the road, the constable snapped his command.

'You've got all this wrong, you know, PC Six-twenty-three.' Here the youth leaned forward to read the number on the constable's epaulettes. 'We ain't done nothing for you ter get so shirty about. It's this old geezer here.' A thumb was prodded at the back of Harry's head. 'He's all uptight just 'cos his loverly little daughter is bein' led astray.' The thumb jabbed again, forcing Harry to jerk his head forward. 'Ain't that right, Pops? 'Course it is—see, he's noddin' his bonce.'

'Save it, son. We'll hear all about it when we get to the nick.' A note approaching boredom edged the constable's voice.

Harry shot him a quick glance, but the profile remained steadily turned, telling him nothing.

As if to compensate for the restriction they'd endured in the cramped back seats of the panda cars, the gang came together with an excess of noise in the wide entrance hall of the police station. They were seeking now to outdo each other in daring as they slapped backs, shook hands and yelled their defiance of authority under the guise of boisterous greeting. Knowing glances were exchanged by the uniformed men, and no time was lost in transferring the gang to an office deep in the bowels of the station.

'Let them sweat it out in there for a while,' was the desk sergeant's comment as he resumed his place behind the high counter.

'How long will you keep them? Will they be detained overnight?' Harry asked. Then, at the sergeant's look of enquiry, explained rather apologetically; 'My daughter . . . she's one of them. Will you . . . will you lock her up?'

'Not unless she's on our wanted for murder list,' came the dry reply.

'Then what happens now? What *will* you do? Are they under arrest?'

'No, we'll give them time to settle down, then we'll ask a few questions. After that — well, we will be turning them out, I should think.'

'You mean you won't be making any charges?'

'Depends. Might be a case of criminal damage, if we can prove malicious intent. Then again it might be we'll just let them go, lacking sufficient evidence.'

'Let them go? But . . . but . . .' Harry didn't know how to receive this information. If it meant Christine could leave without any further stain on her character he'd be the last one to argue. On the other hand, if she was to escape retribution then so would the rest of them, and Harry, along with his neighbours, had suffered too much at their hands to be content with that. The desk sergeant watched the play of emotions across Harry's face with pity, then he cleared his throat, noisily anxious to bring himself and their official surroundings back into the other man's awareness.

Harry's startled recoil gave proof that he had succeeded. 'I . . . er . . . Could I use your phone, do you think?' he asked after a quick glance at the wall clock. 'I wouldn't ask, only, well, it's nearly two o'clock and I forgot to let the wife know I was coming.'

'I expect she'll have guessed,' said the sergeant, passing the telephone across the counter just the same. 'Mothers never need much telling— not in my experience— not where their daughters are concerned, they don't.'

'Oh, but Christine isn't her daughter. Oh Lord! I'd better ring her mother as well, I suppose. Sorry, Sergeant. I can find a phone-box if you'd rather.'

'Might as well use this one, we're not likely to get any busier tonight.'

'Right, thanks. I'll make it as quick as I can,' Harry promised. Joan's angry voice answered after only the third ring and Harry was left in no doubt that she had indeed guessed where he was.

'I don't suppose it has occurred to you that I've been sitting here, waiting up half the night,' she greeted him stormily.

'You should have gone to bed, love.'

'Bed! While you run around, God knows where, after that sly little bitch. I'll tell you straight, Harry, after tonight's revelations she's been here for the last time. If you think—'

'Look, love. I'm ringing from the police station, I'll have to go. See you as soon as I can.' Harry cut across his wife's angry tirade and depressed the phone buttons. A quick glance at the sergeant's bland face gave no indication whether he had heard or guessed Joan's reaction. Taking a deep breath, Harry switched the receiver to his other hand and began to dial once again. This time it took much longer for his call to be answered.

' 'Lo?' The half-word was well wrapped in a sleepy yawn.

'Glenys, it's me — Harry.'

'Who?'

'Me, Harry.'

'Oh, *you*.' There was a digestive pause, then: 'God, Harry. What time is it?'

'About two o'clock. Listen, I'm down at the Shaw Street police station. It's Christine.'

'Chris? Oh no! Harry, she's not . . .'

'She's all right, leastways she's not hurt or anything — Not yet.'

'Not yet? Look, what on earth's going on?'

'I'll have to tell you that when I see you. I'm only ringing to let you know where Christine is. Not that you seem to have missed her a great deal,' he added on a bitter note. 'I'll see she gets home safely when we're through here and we can talk later.' He hung up without giving his ex-wife any chance of further conversation. 'Thanks a lot, Sergeant,' he said, passing the phone back over the counter.

'You might as well sit yourself down.' The sergeant nodded towards the wooden chairs lining the walls of the room. 'Care for a cup of tea?'

'That's very good of you, thanks.' Harry availed himself of a chair and was presented with the promised tea very soon after. Once he'd emptied the cup and had read every one of the many posters for the umpteenth time he ventured to ask: 'I don't suppose you've any idea how much longer?'

Before the sergeant could make any reply a sudden clatter of feet announced the approach of two police constables and their nine charges from one of the tunnel-like corridors opening into the reception area.

Harry got up from his chair and took a hesitant step forward as his daughter came into sight. 'Christine.' The name left his lips barely above a whisper.

'Don't you touch me!' The girl halted, catching hold of the arm of her nearest companion and causing him to pause at her side. 'Don't you bloody well touch me.'

'Christine . . . I . . . look, we can't talk here—not like this.'

The whole gang had halted now and were forming into a half-circle of interested spectators.

'We can't talk anywhere. I've heard enough of your pissy-arsed theories to last me a lifetime.' Her face made ugly by the lips drawn back from her teeth and by the narrowly slitted eyes, Harry's daughter rounded upon him.

'Constable, can't we . . . ?' Harry lifted his hand in helpless appeal to the nearest PC.

'Sorry, sir. Nothing we can do. It's purely a domestic matter now.' The constable had had a long day.

'You're letting them off?'

'Yeah, dey sho's is lettin' us off, white man,' the young Negro shouldered up to Harry. 'What else am dey agoin' ta do, frien', seein' as how inn-o-cent we all is?' The exaggerated Rastafarian speech brought a surge of cheers from his companions.

Ignoring them, his eyes fixed on his daughter, Harry made a fresh appeal. 'Let me see you home, Chris; we can sort this out between us. I didn't realize how you felt . . . I know you didn't mean . . .'

'Oh, I *meant* it all right. Never think for one moment that I didn't. I meant you and that cow you're shacked up with to be scared shitless.'

'Joan is my wife, Christine.' Harry's fists clenched involuntarily, but he kept his temper.

'Wife, is she? And what am I, then?' Christine shrilled. 'Your bastard?'

'Aw, come on. Let's get out of here.' The gang lost interest as the recriminations and excuses threatened to become nothing more exciting than a verbal family battle. They pressed towards the door, forcing Christine along with them.

'No, let go! Leave me be. Let me just tell him since he wants to talk so bad.' She hung back on the hands that were drawing her along and planted herself, legs apart, in front of Harry. 'It's like this, you see, Daddy dear. You got too greedy. You wanted it all — a simpering mug for a daughter who would live quietly out of your way with her mummy and her equally simpering idiot brothers. You wanted no grief, no problems, no demands on your time. And having got all that, you wanted a daughter you could trot out for inspection whenever it suited. A nice goody-goody little girl who'd be a credit to you. Well, it won't wash. I've got rights too, you know. I've got a right to expect my very own father to at least *live* with my very own mother!'

'Chrissy . . . I . . .'

'Don't you Chrissy me, you selfish shit. Next time we won't stop at breaking windows and scratching cars. Next time we'll smash you. *Do you understand me?*' The girl was a girl no longer. Beside herself with an almost manic resentment, she became a twisted, distorted demon, consumed by her own passions.

A silence fell on her audience as they waited for her next onslaught, something forewarning them all of their own inextricable involvement.

'We'll get *her* first. We'll mark her for life — and then we'll come after *you*.'

'Shut up, Chris! Belt up, for Christ's sake.' One of the girl's companions, after glancing apprehensively at their uniformed escort, tried to quell her outburst but she gave no sign of having heard him.

'And after you,' she promised Harry, 'all those

whining, griping slobs that you live among. They know what you are, know what you've done to me and my mum — you and your bloody woman. They deserve all you bring on them.' Christine was sobbing now, her face awash with tears. 'Did they pat your back when we wrecked their gardens? Call you a good sort then, did they? Did they like having you for a neighbour when they discovered all the little tricks we played on them? *Well, did they?*' With a strangled scream the girl hurled herself at her father, fingers hooked and clawing towards his face.

Harry grabbed for her hands but was unable to hold off her demoniacal strength.

The two policemen, freed from their spell of immobilization, moved in to assist Harry, and the gang, aware that all the denials of the past couple of hours were now gone for naught, surged forward, trying as one to get out of the door.

'Not yet, boys. Not yet.' The desk sergeant was there before them, his solid bulk barring their escape. 'Got a bit of explaining to do, haven't you? Come on now, lads, back along the corridor with you, let's try it again, shall we?' As his companionable tone drew the heat from the situation, the push for the door was arrested and the gang fell back, milling around the reception counter until they were turned back towards the interview room.

A policewoman materialized from yet another side-room and took charge of the now subdued and weeping Christine. Harry wiped at the blood welling from the stripes her fingernails had left on his cheeks and fought his own battle to keep his emotions private.

The men, meeting at Trevor's house the following day, discussed Christine's involvement in a sort of disjointed manner as if by not taking the meat from the bones they could pretend her being there last night was merely co-incidental.

'God! Did you see old Harry's face?'

'Wonder what happens next? I mean, will there be a court case?'

'Bound to be.'

'I'd never have thought it possible—not one of your own kids, like.'

'Came as a real smack in the teeth, I thought.'

'Hope they all get ten years.'

'Some hope! They'll probably be told not to be so naughty in future and get let off with a fine. You know how soft the courts are these days.'

'What about Harry's girl? Do you think she—'

No one ever knew what thoughts might have been admitted, for Harry came in through the back door as the question was voiced. He stepped into the room, crowded with his now silent neighbours, and steeled himself to face them. After a brief look at his nail-scarred face they all found their eyes sliding away, avoiding meeting one another's as their embarrassment mounted.

'I . . . er, I . . . What can I say?' Harry forced the words past his lips. 'You've all been made to suffer through my fault, it seems. I . . . I . . .'

Trevor came to his aid. 'Not your fault, Harry,' he said gruffly. 'Hardly that, was it?'

'You weren't at the station last night—or should I say this morning. She, Christine . . . She seems to have been the one putting the rest of them up to it.'

The men digested this in silence until Trevor voiced the question they were all burning to ask. 'But why? What possible reason . . . ?'

'To get back at me. Seems she's got some twisted ideas about the divorce, about me and Joan . . . about me and Glenys, her mother . . .' Harry shrugged helplessly.

'Well, I don't buy that,' said George Turner stoutly. 'A bit of a kid like your girl. How could *she* be responsible for that gang of roughs? More likely *they* put her up to taking the blame.'

'Nice of you to see it like that, George. I only wish it was so, but I heard enough from her last night to convince me . . . God, my very own daughter.' Harry shook his head in disbelief. In speaking the words, he'd heard again the echo of Christine's voice. 'My very own father,' she had said. 'I have rights too—my very own father to live with my very own mother.' Oh, what a mess it all was.

'What else went on? At the station, I mean.' Philip edged closer to Harry; his expression was hard. *His* very own daughter had been forced into the world prematurely because of the things this man's daughter had done. His wife's sanity had been, and still was, at risk. That was going to take some forgiving.

'What else? Not much, they've charged them—I think.' Harry found it difficult to be more positive, caught up as he was with the shock of Christine's defection. She had always been such a sweet child.

'You think?' Brian Goss pressed.

'Well, I'm not sure of the procedure. They took written statements . . . That fellow Philip tangled with seems to be known to them . . . I *did* guess that much . . . Christine refused to see me after . . . after . . .' Harry passed his fingers gingerly along the raw wounds on his cheeks. 'They said quite a bit about gang psychology,' he offered in conclusion.

'Gang psychology! That's just another name for bloody hooliganism. What I'm asking is, are they going to make them pay for all the damage they've done?' Mike Challoner demanded.

'I couldn't tell you. I . . . We'll just have to wait and see. I suppose . . . I'd like to make compensation to all of you. After all—' Harry lifted his shoulders— 'I feel that I should, only . . . well . . . running two homes is very expensive . . . I don't know . . .'

'Oh, for crying out loud, Harry. Don't be so soft. None

of us want to screw you for all this. Forget it, man. What do you say?' Trevor looked around for support and was greeted by only a ragged response. 'Phil?' he appealed and Philip owned rather reluctantly that he felt no grudge against Harry on personal grounds.

'You said the youth I got hold of had a police record?' he asked.

'Oh no. No, I didn't say that, Phil. I said he seemed to be known to the police, that's all.'

'Did you learn his name?'

'Mottershead. Kevin Mottershead. Why?'

'Oh, I might want to look him up sometime, that's all,' Philip said lightly.

'I'd go carefully if I were you,' advised Trevor seriously. 'You could find yourself facing a charge of assault after last night's demonstration.'

'Assault? Me? Are you crazy, after all they've done—'

'Never mind all they've done. I'm telling you, Philip. That youth could charge you with assault for what you did.'

'How come you know so much all at once?' Philip bristled at his friend.

'I looked it up. When all the plans for getting to grips with the gang ourselves were first mooted.'

'I see. Then try looking up how long I'll get if I murder him, because if anything more happens to Ann or the baby through those parasites, that's exactly what I'll do.'

'Hey, steady on, steady on,' George advised. 'Let's not fall out with each other after all we've been through together.'

Philip had the grace to look apologetic. 'Sorry, Trev,' he mumbled. 'George's right. I think I'm letting all this get to me.'

'Aren't we all?' A supportive voice asked from the depths of an armchair.

'Yes, I'm afraid we are. And now I suggest we let the

subject drop and leave it all in police hands. No doubt they will let us know what develops. Come on, Harry, I've given Dawn the day off and sent her off to her mother's, so you can give me a hand to open some beer-cans,' said Trevor, having the last word for once.

If the residents of Lynden Grove were content to leave the matter there, the local press were not. A reporter toured the Grove, knocking on doors, asking questions, making notes, examing evidence of damage and making a nuisance of himself in general. How he'd become alerted to the situation no one was able to discover, nor who gave him all the details he subsequently acquired, but the newspaper's headlines for that week's edition of the local *Advertiser* informed its readers of the spanking administered to the youth they termed 'One more product of our uncaring society.'

Philip was vastly entertained by the article. 'That'll show them, and any more of their ilk, where they get off,' he told Trevor when they met across at Trevor's home the following weekend.

'I don't know, Phil. Things like this article sometimes have very nasty repercussions,' was Trevor's guarded reply.

'Oh, come on, don't be such an old woman,' Dawn put in impatiently. 'I'd say it's just what's needed. Nothing like a spot of ridicule for taking that sort of slob down a peg or two.'

'That sort of slob, Dawn, is often dangerously unbalanced. Push them too far and there's no telling what they might do. You've only to look at Harry's experience, for one.'

Philip shifted uneasily. There was a weary note in Trevor's voice that told of frequent quarrels on this very same subject, and the atmosphere between husband and wife appeared strained.

Dawn glared at Trevor's averted head. 'Suit yourself,' she snapped as she flounced out of the room.

'I, er, I'll get off to the nursing home.' Philip tried to speak naturally, as if he'd missed the underlying anger. 'Ann's making much better progress—should have her home in a couple of days.'

'That's good news, Phil. What of the baby?'

'Gaining weight, and beginning to look more human, thank God.'

'Does Ann know anything about all this?' Trevor flicked the newspaper.

'Lord, no. No, and she's not to find out. I told her all this business was cleared up weeks ago. It could set her right back if she was to see that story.'

Trevor gave his friend a long, measured look. 'Then for heaven's sake, Phil, try to avoid raking it all up again.'

'Raking it up? I've no intention—'

'That's okay, then, only I thought . . . Well, never mind what I thought, let's say no more about it. Give Ann our love and tell her we are looking forward to seeing her home.'

Philip breezed towards the outer door. 'I'll be sure and do that small thing. 'Bye then, for now.'

CHAPTER 9

Philip's optimistic hopes regarding Ann's discharge from Green Lawns were confirmed. 'Come and collect her about two o'clock tomorrow afternoon, Mr Butler,' Sister advised. 'She'll have seen the doctor and learned the arrangements for her out-patient treatment by that time.'

'Out-patient? But I thought she was better.'

'So she is, she is. Don't let the thought of further treatment alarm you. We just want to keep an eye on her for a week or two, that's all.'

'I see,' said Philip without real conviction. He didn't truly 'see' any of this. Didn't see why this nightmare should be happening to them. Didn't see why they should have been singled out in this way. Didn't see what harm either Ann or he had done anyone to deserve this sort of retribution.

'She'll be perfectly all right, you know.' The sister had faced this reaction many times and was becoming adept at reading minds. 'Just take her home, give her lots of love and understanding, and she'll be as good as new.'

'I hope so, Sister. Anyway, I'll certainly do as you say,' Philip promised as he took his leave.

'Then take that look of doubt off your face, for a start,' she called after him, and was reassured by the grin he awarded her.

In spite of his brave resolutions Ann's homecoming was not quite as happy as Philip could have wished. She was hesitant and unsure, a timid echo of her former self, her exclamation of delight at seeing the changes he had made in the hall somewhat overshadowed by the aura of a visiting guest that seemed to cling about her.

'Go on in and sit down, I'll make us a cup of tea.' Philip opened the lounge door and ushered Ann over the threshold. She stepped into the room and stood looking about her in an uncertain manner.

'Shall I get the tea, Philip?' she asked, without giving any indication she was willing to do so.

'No, no. You take your coat off and make yourself comfortable. I'm head cook and bottle-washer for today.'

Ann's consenting grimace was a pale travesty of her old infectious smile. Philip returned to the kitchen, where he ran the tap and filled the kettle with automatic precision. He was spooning the tea into the pot when Ann's cry of dismay took him swiftly to her side. 'What is it, love? Whatever's the matter?'

Ann was staring through the front window, her gaze fixed on the FOR SALE board in Dawn and Trevor's garden. 'Oh, Philip.' She turned to him with a little pleading gesture. 'Why?'

'Something to do with Trev's job, darling—can't be helped. We'll miss them, I expect,' he lied convincingly.

'It's not . . . not . . . they're . . . Oh, Philip, it is all right now, isn't it?'

'Of course it is. I promise you. All our troubles are over in that direction at least.' Correctly interpreting her fears, he caught her to him and hugged her protectively. 'Don't start fretting, darling. The gang wars are finished. I knew you'd be upset about Dawn and Trev leaving and that's the only reason I didn't tell you before. There's nothing sinister about it, honestly.' He felt her begin to relax against his chest.

'I'm sorry,' she said in a small voice. 'I'll try not to be so silly.'

'Hmm,' said Philip, 'I've heard that one before.' He kissed the top of her head. 'And the next time you see a spider you'll be throwing yourself at me again, you shameless hussy.'

Ann managed a giggle. 'You should be so lucky,' she told him with a flash of her old humour as she disentangled herself from his arms. And Philip was persuaded that the nursing sister had been right after all—just give things a little time and all would be well.

Dawn and Trevor came across to welcome Ann home, bringing their two boys with them as previously arranged. As Philip had hoped, Ann seemed to draw comfort from their presence. She knew it had been the practice for them to spend the weekends with their grandparents in the past months and the fact that they were still home on a Saturday night did more to convince her that the raids they'd all dreaded were now at an end than any amount of verbal reassurance from Philip and their friends.

'Wait until you get the baby home,' Dawn teased. 'You won't be so pleased to see other people's kids then. What with bottles and bibs, lines full of nappies and nights without sleep, you'll be wishing them all a hundred miles away. I know I did when these two were small.'

'Ah, but I'm going to rope you in as babysitter-in-chief.' Ann responded to her friend's humour with all her returning confidence.

'Wish you'd tell that to my pig-headed husband, then, before he has us moving to the back of beyond with his schoolgirl timidity!' The bitterness in Dawn's tone came across clearly, startling Ann and bringing Trevor to his feet in protest. Dawn realized too late the effect her ill-considered remark was having on Ann, who was now staring at her with a mixture of doubt and concern on her face. 'Look, I'm sorry. Forget I said that,' she begged. 'I didn't mean to upset you.'

'Come on, Dawn, we'd better be going. Ann doesn't want to get involved in our quarrels.' Trevor was apologetic.

'No! Don't go. Tell me about it,' Ann invited. 'Why *are* you leaving—really, Dawn?' She began to pick nervously at her fingers. In spite of her brave words her eyes grew wary, something in her manner making her appear poised for flight like some shy woodland creature.

'Oh, take no notice of me, Ann. You know how I run on when I get ratty. We're leaving because Trevor wants to try a new job and I'm not really in favour, that's all.' Dawn pushed her resentment aside in a sincere attempt to convince her friend that all was well. They had agreed between them, she, Philip and Trevor, to stick to the story that the move was planned simply because Trevor was changing his job, only her personal discontent with the situation had caused her to speak out, forgetting the role she'd determined to play.

'I didn't know Daddy had a new job.' Mark, the Austins'

six-year-old, chose this moment to join in the conversation of his elders.

'Well, we don't tell *you* everything, young man.' Trevor hurried to forestall any further comment from his sons. 'Nor you, buster.' Here he poked his finger into young David's ribs, hitting unerringly on a ticklish spot. The child gurgled and folded up.

' 'Gain, Daddy. Do it again,' he pleaded, a broad smile stretching across his rosy face. The tension was eased from the situation, and Philip breathed a quick sigh of relief as he saw Ann's trembling hands begin to relax and watched the spark of alarm die from her eyes. He felt confident enough then to give her a slow wink before pursing his lips in the direction of the two children, the accompanying shake of his head implying the subject was taboo only because of *their* presence.

The remainder of the weekend passed, if not happily, at least a little more comfortably, and it wasn't until Monday morning that Philip's private intention of learning more about the youth Kevin Mottershead brought Ann's newly won confidence once again to the brink of disaster. She had insisted upon getting up with him and fixing his breakfast.

'I'm not going to be treated like an invalid any longer,' she said firmly, feeding two rounds of bread into the toaster. 'I'm quite capable of seeing to things for myself now, thank you. And anyway, I will jolly soon have to be, won't I? We'll be bringing Melanie home any day now.'

Philip felt a rush of relief. At last she was talking in a normal manner about their child—acknowledging her existence without any prompting. Things were going along just fine, as the medical people had predicted. Ann really was going to make a full recovery. He rose from the breakfast-table and pulled her into his arms.

'Come and give your old man a kiss and a squeeze,

then,' he commanded, and Ann returned his kiss with spontaneous warmth.

The click from the toaster as the hot toast popped up brought them back to the mundane awareness of Monday-morning work schedules. 'Oh, you'll be late if I don't get a move on. Sit down, darling, do.' Ann heaped scrambled eggs on to the toast and placed it in front of Philip. 'Now, where's your sandwich box?' She caught up the polythene box and peeled back the fitted lid. A neatly folded square of greaseproof paper and a somewhat ragged piece of news-paper fluttered to the table as she up-ended the box. 'What's this?' she asked as she reached for the printed page. Philip looked up at her question and made a belated grab for the cutting.

'It's nothing, Ann. Just an article I — '

'Philip!' The agonized exclamation, coupled with Ann's instinctive recoil, stopped the words in his throat. Slow colour climbed into his face, a feeling of guilt holding him immobile as he watched Ann read the rather exagger-ated details of his part in the head-to-head clash with the vandals.

At last she lowered the cutting and turned on him a look of accusation mixed with total disbelief. 'Oh no, Phil. No . . . How *could* you?'

Guilt and regret made him brusque. 'How could I? How could I not, don't you mean? Give me the cutting, please.' He took it from her nerveless fingers. 'And don't stare at me like that. You wanted them stopped, didn't you?'

'But not like this. Not this way. Oh Philip, can't you see what you've done? You have descended to their level. It says here that . . . that you tipped him over your knee and gave him a spanking — a *spanking*, Phil. To a grown man, almost.'

'And you think I shouldn't have?' For a moment Philip forgot that this was his wife — the wife who had been so ill and confused — the wife he should be protecting against any upset like this. 'What would you have me do? Kiss his bloody feet?' Ann raised a hand to her lips, the tears of weakness flooding her eyes, and Philip's anger drained away. 'I'm sorry, love. I didn't mean that. Please . . . Please, darling, don't turn away.'

He was too late, Ann was already out of the room.

'Aw, well, *go*, then. See if I care.' He slammed his way about the kitchen, tossed the sandwiches Ann had prepared for his lunch into the box, and jerked on his jacket with a force calculated to tear the sleeve from its socket. He marched through the hall, out of the front door and round to the garage, where he flung up the door and bounced into the car.

Ann heard the engine start. The squeal of the tyres as he backed furiously along the drive and out on to the road gave her an indication as to his temper. Clutching his pyjama jacket to her chest, she buried her face in its still warm folds and wept tears of apprehension.

By the time he reached the office most of Philip's ill humour had fled and he was beginning to feel remorse for having vented it upon Ann. I think I'll have a run home at lunch-time, see if she's okay — maybe give her a lift into town, she might like to do a bit of shopping. He salved his conscience with the thought, then gave his mind to the intricate problems of assessing the seemingly endless pile of cases on his desk. The strike action having petered out the previous week, all personnel were once again working within the department, and facing with some depression the backlog that had built up during their absence. Case after case was assessed, annotated and passed to Helen Broadhurst for authorization of payment.

'Stop! Stop.' Pushing her chair away from her desk, Helen jumped to her feet, raising protesting hands as she faced the men working at the desks alongside her own.

'Enough is enough, you lot. Come on, all of you — let's to coffee.'

Clutching the back of his neck, easing cramped muscles with a circular motion of his head, Philip gazed up at her. 'And why not?' he responded to her suggestion with an enthusiastic grin.

Long after their colleagues had drifted back to their desks they were sitting together in the small upstairs room that did duty as a canteen. Philip pushed aside his empty cup and absent-mindedly dabbled his index finger in the ring of moisture it had left behind on the formica-topped table. Trailing a wet comet along in the wake of his finger, he found himself spelling out the name Mottershead. Helen screwed herself around in her seat opposite, trying to read the badly formed letters. 'Mother?' she guessed aloud at the first T. 'M-O-T-T-E-R. Motter? What's that?'

'Mottershead,' replied Philip, suddenly losing patience and scrubbing away the letters with the side of his hand. Helen shot him a questioning glance. 'He's the swine that I clouted last week.'

'Oh, *him*. He's not been round again, has he?'

'No. At least, not in the flesh. He reared his ugly mug over my breakfast table this morning, though. Via the good offices of the local press.'

'Eh?'

'I kept the bloody cutting, put it in my snap tin, then forgot it was there. Ann found it.'

'Oh no! Was she upset?'

'You *could* say that,' Philip replied lightly in an attempt to take the sting from the memory of Ann's stricken face. But her expression continued to haunt him. 'Oh hell, yes! Yes, she was very upset, and I didn't make things any better . . . I'd like to break his bloody neck,' he added through clenched teeth.

'How did you come by his name? I noticed the press

were careful not to print that sort of detail about your playmates — even though you and your neighbours were given full billing. 'Spect that was because of the pending case, was it?'

'I don't really know, I suppose so. I found out because Har — I, er . . .' Philip was suddenly reminded that Helen's brother was a police officer. Wouldn't do to let on about Harry's disclosure, it might have repercussions. 'One of the chaps down the road recognized him,' he ended lamely.

'Oh, I see. I'll bet he's one of ours, then,' said Helen with a grimace of distaste. 'All the well-known faces end up here.'

'Yeah. That's why I hung on to the newspaper cutting — to remind me. I intended looking through the files and giving any Mottershead the once-over.'

'Hmm, bit dangerous that, Phil. After all, there's nothing you can do now, better leave it to the police.'

'To do what, exactly? Let 'em off with a caution?'

'But didn't you say the whole thing blew up because of a neighbour's quarrel with his daughter? Surely you don't expect any further trouble.'

'I don't know. Christine may have been the main instigator, but the rest of them certainly enjoyed it.' He was in a mood to argue.

'And isn't that rather what you're doing now?' asked Helen gently.

'Aw, come on. We've lived under the strain of their bloody attacks for months. My wife's been driven to the edge of insanity, our baby's been born two months prematurely, our best friends have been practically forced out of their home — and you say I've enjoyed it?'

'No, no, I didn't, Philip. I said, or rather implied, that you are enjoying it *now*, now you've gained the whip hand.' Helen rose from the table and stood looking down on him. 'Think about it, Phil. Don't get drawn into anything you'll regret,' she cautioned before turning to leave.

Philip gave her advice only brief consideration. Helen and her brother were very close, no doubt his indoctrination with law and order had rubbed off on her. Perhaps she'd feel differently if ever she found herself on the receiving end for a change, was his sour reflection.

Determined now to pursue his investigation of Kevin Mottershead as far as he could, Philip quit the canteen and entered the filing section, where he ploughed through the alpha-filing system. M-Mo-Mott — Got it! — Mottershead K. His pulse raced as he prised the dog-eared file from the closely packed drawer. Assuming for the benefit of the clerks dotted about the room a nonchalance he was far from feeling, he slapped it on the top of the filing cabinet and rifled through the information it contained. Yes, this was his man all right. A history of unemployment since leaving school, a three-month spell in a detention centre, plus two linked cases — his father and brother; this couldn't be coincidental, it had to be the same youth. Searching through the numerous reports and assessments, Philip located the current payment sheet and noted the signing-on day. Thursday morning. Right; come next Thursday the local Employment Exchange were to be honoured with a personal visit. He would call round there on the pretext of checking out some payment or other and hang around until he had a chance to get a good look at Mr Kevin Mottershead, just to confirm that the character described in those files, and the louse he'd had over his knee, were one and the same.

He drove home at lunch-time in a more settled frame of mind, intent upon making up his quarrel with Ann, and was alarmed to find the house empty. With panic mounting, he strode through the rooms calling her name. Where could she be if not here? She had no appointments that he knew of, had made no arrangements to be away from home. Surely their tiff this morning hadn't been serious enough to . . . Here Philip shut his mind to the accusing, fear-provoking voice that told him Ann still wasn't strong, was in fact still very finely balanced. He refused even to consider the possibility of her doing anything 'silly' and found himself instead rather foolishly going through the clothes hanging in her wardrobe. With part of his mind he acknowledged that unless Ann was to empty the hangers completely he would have no real idea whether she had removed any of her clothes or not. Damn, damn, damn. He sat himself on the edge of the bed with a spine-jarring thump. Where the devil was she? He checked his watch. He had only twenty minutes before he must start back to the office. He wasted several minutes in fruitless irritation before it suddenly occurred to him to check with Dawn. She might have seen Ann go out — or Ann could even be across at Dawn's place having a coffee or something.

There was no response to his knock at Dawn's front door, and he was returning along the side of the house from his attempt to gain answer at the back when he heard Dawn calling to him from along the road. She was struggling along under the load of several heavy baskets, obviously returning home from a morning's shopping. She was alone. Philip hurried to relieve her of some of her burden, asking after Ann as he did so.

'Oh, she left about an hour after you,' Dawn told him. 'She's gone to see the baby. Didn't you know?'

Of course; the baby. Philip groaned aloud, clapping a hand to his head at his lack of foresight. God, what an idiot. How could he have overlooked that possibility? 'I must be going round the twist,' he said with a relieved grin at Dawn. 'I've had her under a bus, full of barbiturates and twice in the river, but never once did I think of the obvious.'

'Under a bus? Good heavens, Phil. She's not . . . not . . .

She's all right now, isn't she? I mean there's no chance . . .'

'Oh yes, yes. Of course she's fine, only we had a bit of a spat this morning, my fault of course, I was forgetting how ill she'd been. She found out about last Saturday's rumpus and I made things worse . . . Still, if she's gone to see the baby she must be feeling okay.'

'Did you come home purposely? To make up, like?'

'Well, sort of. But never mind as long as she's okay.'

'Come and have a coffee with me, then — you've got time, haven't you?'

Philip eyed Dawn a little dubiously. There had been a decided change in their relationship recently, what with Trevor's attitude to the move and Ann's illness, he and Dawn were finding themselves being pushed together. And while he was quite happy at this point, he felt a shade wary of getting in any deeper. On the other hand, Dawn certainly shared his feelings about creeps like Kevin Mottershead; it would be a relief to talk to someone about him without being soft-pedalled all the time; he'd had enough of that first with Ann and next with Helen Broad-hurst. 'Okay, then.' He swung the basket he carried in a jaunty arc. 'Just lead the way, MacDuff!'

CHAPTER 10

Philip was careless on his visit to the Employment Ex-change. An insurmountable anger as he recognized the heavy black brows, the straggling beard and the sneering attitude of the youth he'd grown to hate propelled him forward into Mottershead's line of vision. For a second they stared into each other's eyes, naked hatred sparking between them. Philip hadn't intended this to happen; to see while remaining unseen had been the plan. He had no real business here, not in the public section, and he didn't want to create any trouble within the department over his private vendetta. He tore his gaze from the slouching figure, but the gleam of gold from the gipsy earring and the glint of steel from the studded black jacket burned a clear impression on the retina of his eye.

Making a hurried excuse to the nearest counter clerk, he picked up the sheaf of papers he'd brought with him as camouflage and made a hasty exit. His only hope of escaping retribution lay in the possibility of Mottershead accepting his presence here as official; even then he might make waves by implying unfair collusion between government departments. Blast! Why hadn't he listened to Helen and been content to leave well alone? He scurried back to his office and threw himself into an orgy of paperwork, hoping against hope that he'd hear no more of his escapade.

His hopes were doomed to be very short-lived. One of the clerical assistants passing through the assessment section tapped his shoulder as she passed. 'Arise, Sir Philip,' she intoned solemnly. 'His Nibs the URO requests the pleasure.'

Philip's heart plunged. The Unemployment Review Officer — URO for short — was a creature apart. A senior officer appointed to keep a constant watch on all able-bodied people regularly signing for employment benefit, he was known throughout the region as a hard-hitting no-nonsense disciplinarian. Rumour had it that he was totally devoid of all human feeling, and Philip would have been the last to quarrel with that.

'Ho, ho! Summoned to the Kremlin,' Helen twitted him. 'You're doomed for Siberia, my lad.'

'It's all a dirty Communist plot,' Philip retorted, doing his best to keep up his end of the comedy while trying to overcome the sharp twinges of apprehension that fired his insides. He started out of the room reluctantly, wishing himself anywhere but his present situation.

The URO lost no time in pleasantries. He fixed Philip with a steely gaze and demanded to know what business had taken him round to the Employment Exchange.

'I had a payment figure I wanted to check.' The lie sounded hollow even to Philip.

' 'Phone out of order, then, is it?'

'N-no, I . . . it was a bit complicated, a benefit suspension thing . . . I thought it would be easier to do it in person.'

'Wasn't a payment for Kevin Mottershead, by any chance?'

Philip chose not to answer that. A slow flush mounted his cheeks under the senior man's penetrating gaze.

'Let's get it clear, Butler. This is a government department — not the Mafia. If you have any axes to grind with Mottershead or anyone else you'll oblige me by not doing so while you're supposedly working.'

'I said nothing to Mottershead. If he's claiming I did he's lying.'

'He's not lying when he claims that you were round at the Exchange simply to check up on him though, is he? *Nor* when he claims that you are abusing your position in this department to gain information that may be to his detriment.' The angry spate ceased while the URO scrutinized the figure standing guiltily before him. 'You bloody young fool,' he said, on a more personal note. 'Don't you realize that he's got you by the cobblers? He's only got to trot this out in court and any case you may have against him would go straight down the pan. Not to mention the fact that if the Chief gets to hear about this morning's escapade your job could be in jeopardy.'

Philip shuffled his feet and squirmed inwardly as he acknowledged the truth of all that was said. 'I'm sorry. I didn't stop to think . . . I . . . You see—'

'Yes, as a matter of fact I do see. I see the local rag every week, same as the rest of the staff in this department, so you can spare me the details.' The weary tones interrupted Philip's floundering explanation. 'Go and get on with your work. I'll do what I can to smooth this thing over — only remember: any more Big Brother tactics from you and I'll chop you off at the knees and send you out with a tin cup.'

Philip stared at the man in amazement before stammering, 'Yes — no. I mean, right. Right, I will, thanks.' The chap must be human after all, he thought as he all but fell out of the door in his hurry to get away. Human indeed, after all that. Or was he? Philip slowed to a halt and stared back along the corridor at the closed door. Perhaps he'd really meant his threat to be taken literally. With a grin at the picture that thought conjured up, he resumed his pace and was still smiling to himself as he gained his own desk.

'So it's not the salt mines?' Helen said, noting his expression.

'Not this time,' was all the explanation he gave. He settled himself behind his desk and opened a case-paper, giving every appearance of total immersion in his work. But his brain was not juggling figures and his eyes did not see the report in front of him. He was miles away, gazing inwards over the events of the past couple of days. How stupid to let his anger take him over in that way; he had quarrelled with Ann, risked his job, given Mottershead just cause for complaint, and all for what? You'd better take a good look at yourself, my lad, he thought ruefully. Ann had been perfectly right when she'd said he had brought himself down to the level of those hooligans, and it was high time he put the whole destructive business behind him and concentrated instead on building a happy, secure future for his wife and child.

It was as well that Philip recovered himself when he did, for the next few weeks presented him with ample opportunity for revenge had he so wished. It began with a visit from a very changed, very apologetic Harry Knight. He arrived on Philip's doorstep one Sunday evening with a bottle of sherry which he presented to Ann in a diffident manner. 'Just a small token,' he muttered as she took it from him with a puzzled expression. 'Least I can do, not enough, not nearly enough, but . . .'

'Harry, I'm sorry . . . I . . .' Ann clutched the bottle and looked towards Philip for support; maybe *he* knew what this was all about?

Philip felt, rather than saw, Harry's abject misery, and with a swift rush of compassion, not untinged with shame for his own previously begrudging attitude towards the man, extended his hand towards him.

Rather hesitantly Harry responded, but the strength and warmth of Philip's handshake left him in no doubt that here at least he was not being censured for his daughter's behaviour. His eyes filled and he blinked vigorously. 'I . . . Phil . . . I . . .' He produced his handkerchief and blew his nose. 'Thanks, Phil,' he managed to say. 'It's very good of you.'

'Rubbish! Now come on in and let's try a drop of that sherry. It looks good enough to drink,' Philip said, attempting to put Harry at his ease.

'Are you sure? I mean . . .'

'Look, Harry, I don't blame you for what happened. I don't even blame Christine particularly.'

'Then you're more generous than some—including my wife.' In the relief of finding someone he could talk to Harry gave his depression full rein and made no further resistance as Philip steered him towards the sitting-room.

'I'm taking no credit, Harry, I'm not proud of the way I reacted, 'specially at first. Only what with Ann and the baby . . . it wasn't easy to keep on an even keel . . . but, well, it's over now, and . . .' He shrugged in dismissal of his former vindictive anger.

Ann rewarded him with the warmest smile she'd managed since her return home. 'Oh Philip,' she said, hugging the bottle of sherry to her chest in an excess of feeling.

'Hey! Get the glasses, woman. The glasses. I don't keep you in luxury to have you standing about in idleness,' he twitted, suddenly riding on cloud nine, with his faith in the good of their future bubbling up to spill over and embrace Harry. 'Don't look so down, old man,' he felt moved to encourage. 'Now that the raids have stopped things will soon get back to normal. People forget.'

'Not very quickly, they don't. And this has just about finished me and Joan. She'd made Chris and her brothers welcome for my sake and now . . . well, now she says she'll kill her if she ever shows her face.' Harry shook his head slowly. 'I can't understand it, Phil. I thought I had it sewn up with those kids. I never let them run wild, always made sure they did as they were told, Christine especially . . . How could she do this?' Harry spread expressive hands.

'It must be the crowd she's got in with. You know how it is.'

'No.' Harry shook his head. 'No, it goes deeper than that, I'm afraid. She said some terrible things . . . And when I tackled her mother about her behaviour she calmly informed me that she'd been expecting something of the sort for a long time.'

'Then why on earth didn't she tell you? Before, I mean, while there was still time for you to do something about it?'

'That's what I asked. But she said something about my having to reap what I had sown, or some such rubbish.'

Ann turned from the sideboard where she'd been pouring the drinks to ask hesitantly, 'Were you and Joan, um . . . Did you leave her . . . Christine's mother, to, er, well . . .'

'To go off with Joan?' Harry reluctantly rescued her

from her red-cheeked embarrassment. 'I, er, I suppose . . . Well, yes. I suppose some people might look at it that way. But things had reached a pretty bad pass before I made any move.' He took the proffered glass absently, his eyes fixed on the blank wall facing his chair as if seeing the past re-enacted on its surface. 'We were at each other's throats all the time, Glenys and me. I stuck it as long as I could, but having the children only served to make things worse. She was always tired, I was always working, and when I was home we were picking and sniping at each other. In the end I simply cleared out. I'd been friendly with Joan for some time, so . . .' His shrug was expressive. 'I paid her, though,' he added swiftly, looking from Ann to Philip, anxious to justify himself. 'Still do, come to that. They've never gone short, neither her nor the kids. And that's what is sticking in Joan's craw; she's a lot younger than me, as you know, she'd have liked a family of her own . . . There was no way we could afford to start up a nursery . . .' Busy with his thoughts, Harry fell silent. Philip and Ann exchanged an understanding glance and made no effort to break in on his brown study. 'I always held Christine and her brothers up to Joan, you know,' he ventured after some time had passed. 'That's part of the trouble. I pushed them at her, tried to make her accept them in place of kids of her own, kept on at her about how well they had turned out . . . Well, she's got the laugh on me now, and no mistake.'

'Oh, Harry, I'm sure Joan doesn't look at it like that,' Ann exclaimed sympathetically. 'She is bound to feel let down, I expect, same as you do yourself. And you can hardly blame her for that, but I'm sure she won't hold Christine's mischief against you. Not once she's had time to get over the shock and look at things in perspective.'

'I only hope you are right.' Harry drained his glass in a swallow and rose to take his leave, 'But I've got my doubts. I think Christine has got what she wanted; she's destroyed us all right, me and Joan, the friendships we'd made around here, there'll be nothing left now . . . nothing.'

Philip showed Harry out and sought desperately for a few words that would give the older man some crumb of comfort. Somehow, there didn't seem anything appropriate, and he could only watch mutely from the front step as Harry trod slowly along the drive and let himself out of the gate on to the street. He turned once as he started along the pavement towards his own home to lift his hand in a gesture of farewell that was at the same time a wave acknowledging defeat. Philip closed the door and returned to the sitting-room to find Ann standing in the middle of the hearth, wine-glass in hand, a worried expression on her face.

'Oh Phil. That poor man. He looked so beaten.'

'I know. It's a hell of a thing. He was so proud of those kids. Seems strange somehow that he could ever walk out on them.' He paused to consider a new train of thought. 'Maybe young Christine had some justification for what she's done after all.'

The case against Christine and her fellow conspirators came up in the Magistrate's Court ten days after Harry's visit. Philip had taken the day off from work to go along to the hearing, as had Trevor, Harry, George and several more of their neighbours. Mindful of his own ignominious visit to the Employment Exchange, Philip viewed the possible revelations with something approaching dread; if Mottershead had been incensed enough to make a complaint to the URO, there was every possibility that he would do the same for the benefit of the magistrates, and the only defence he felt able to offer was a rather childish spite. 'Aw, hell,' he complained to Trevor as they motored together towards the courts, 'this would happen now, just when Ann is showing such improvement. If things go wrong it could set her right back; why on earth did I have to be so bloody stupid?'

'Well, at least you recognize that you were. Small comfort, I know, but it's something to build on, Phil. You'll not do the same thing again.'

'You've said it! But how do I wriggle out of today's little episode?'

'You don't. You'll just have to hope that you are not the only one that's seen the light.' Trevor pulled up in front of the court and switched off the engine. 'Cheer up, maybe Mottershead will be satisfied with his attempt to stir things up for you at work,' he said as he got out of the car. 'He's had time to cool off too, you know.'

'Huh! I can always live in hope if I die in despair,' replied Philip grimly.

As it happened, neither man was prepared for the vitriolic hatred that poured from Kevin Mottershead's bearded lips. Every filthy, indecent obscenity ever voiced came flooding across the court in Philip's direction, loathsome and vile, it tainted the air in its passage until the youth was forcibly quelled by a uniformed officer.

Into the awesome silence that followed the outburst Philip released a shuddering breath, and, turning from left to right, saw mirrored in every man's face the same expression of shock. The remainder of the hearing passed in a hushed manner, as though the principals in the drama were merely stage characters acting out their parts, reading prescribed lines of conciliatory dialogue. A tug at Philip's arm brought him back to an awareness of the happenings about him.

'C'mon. We can go now,' Trevor informed him.

'Eh? . . . Oh!' He stood, and began to shuffle along the narrow space between the rows of seats, following in Trevor's wake like an ambulant sleepwalker. As he reached the end of the row an animal scream brought the clatter of feet to a halt. Mottershead fought blindly with his captors, the scream issuing from his lips turning to a snarl as his gaze fell on Philip.

'You'll pay for this, you bastard. You arse-licking prick! I'll get you! I'll get you!'

Philip returned his stare, stunned anew by the violence of his rage.

'Come on. Let's get out of here.' Trevor grabbed him by the shoulder and tugged him hurriedly out of the court. 'God love us, Philip. You've stirred a hornets' nest there, I think he's insane!'

George Turner, hurrying to catch up with the swift-pacing pair, voiced similar sentiments between his gasps for breath. 'If ever he gets his hands on you, Phil, he'll bloody well kill you.'

Philip strode along, matching his steps to Trevor's, seeing nothing, hearing nothing but Mottershead's voice screaming his threats.

'He's going to spend the next six months cursing you all right,' George went on with relish. 'Talk about a short, sharp shock. He'll get that right enough where he's going. And he'll blast your eyes for every single day of it.'

'Where? Where is he going?' Philip halted his pace so abruptly that George cannoned into his shoulder.

'What? You can't mean to say you missed that bit.' His neighbour looked at him strangely. 'Hey! I think this has all been too much for you. You look lousy.'

Trevor halted and retraced his footsteps to join them. He flicked a glance at Philip's drawn face. 'Are you okay?' he asked.

'Yeah. Yeah, I'm fine. Just a bit queasy.'

'I'm not surprised. I'd be a bit queasy myself with that animal after me,' George told him with feeling. 'And he is certainly going to come, you mark my words. It would take more than the new Borstal to stop the likes of him.'

'Oh, knock it off, can't you.' Trevor rounded on him. 'He's not going after anybody for the next six months, and it will all have blown over by the time he gets released.'

'Sorry I spoke, I'm sure.' George flushed at the rebuke, gave Trevor a hard stare and marched off, leaving him and Philip standing outside the courthouse.

'Are you sure you are all right?' Trevor asked again.

'Yes, thanks.' Philip made an effort to recover himself. 'Let's get home, Ann will be anxious to know how things went — only don't tell her all the details, whatever you do,' he cautioned unnecessarily. 'Where's Harry, by the way?' He looked around at the bustle of people leaving the courts, but failed to spot their neighbour among them.

'He stayed behind, probably having a word with his daughter. She was lucky to get off as she did, twelve months' probation doesn't seem a lot in the face of all the misery she's helped to cause. It's all right for them to claim she was influenced by Mottershead, but who motivated him in the first place if it wasn't her?'

'What about Mottershead? I'm sorry, I wasn't taking a lot of notice.'

'Oh well, he's a real head-case, isn't he? Seems as though he really enjoyed his reign of terror. Hitler was never short of followers either.' Trevor droned on, talking more for the sake of giving Philip time to shake off the numbing effects of Mottershead's verbal attack than to impart any information.

'Well, he will get all he's asked for out at the new place, it's pretty tough from all I hear. Trouble is, Trev, I can't help feeling responsible for most of his malice.'

'Too late to worry now. And anyway, he let you off light when you think about it. He obviously hadn't mentioned your presence at the Employment Exchange to anyone that mattered, so what are a few mindless threats? He'll think better of them when he's had time to cool down, you'll see.'

'I suppose so.' Philip seated himself in Trevor's car and considered his mollifying words. 'Yes, yes, of course you are right, if he'd really wanted to get at me he had every opportunity before today—why should he wait?'

In spite of his attempt at self-assurance Philip was careful to pass none of Mottershead's threats on to Ann. 'It's all over now, love,' he told her in reply to her anxious questions. 'Harry's girl got bound over, along with most of the others.'

'And the other one? The one you . . . You know. What about him?'

'He got six months in the new Borstal.'

'But why? Why, if the others only got bound over? I mean, he wasn't the ringleader, was he—not if Christine put him up to it?'

'Not primarily, no. But he's already got a police record, don't forget. And anyway it seems that only the suggestion came from Harry's daughter. He's the one that got the gang together and organized the whole thing.'

'Why should he? What did he have against us? What are he and Christine to each other?'

'Who's to say? Christine won't. Maybe some sort of teenage crush, maybe nothing at all. Might just be a case of like drawing like, you know how it is, love. Anyway, it seems he enjoyed masterminding "Operation Lynden Grove" for as long as it lasted, but it's over now, so let's put it behind us, shall we?'

'With pleasure, sir.' She dimpled at him secretively. 'I have much better things to think of just now in any case.'

'Like what, madam?' Philip tilted her chin with his finger and gazed fondly down at her suddenly glowing face.

'Like Melanie Jane coming home tomorrow,' she told him in great excitement. 'Oh Philip. Won't it be lovely to have all our troubles over at last?'

CHAPTER 11

The baby's homecoming marked a new chapter in Ann and Philip's lives. Although now topping the scales at five pounds one and a half ounces, she was still very small and peculiarly vulnerable.

'She reminds me of a fledgling,' said Philip, hanging over the side of the cot and gently teasing at the minute hand with his finger. 'Don't you think so? So tiny and boneless, and — and naked somehow.'

'She's not naked!' said Ann indignantly.

'No, but you know what I mean. And anyway, you could hardly call this gown thing a good fit. There's room for two of her in there.'

'Oh, she'll soon fill out.'

Philip smiled to himself, content as he'd not been for months at the complacent certainty in Ann's tone. He straightened up to watch her as she busily folded napkins, laying them to air by the hearth. She had regained all her old bloom in the past couple of days and now seemed set for a full recovery. Just give her a chance now to forget, Philip breathed in silent prayer, and don't let Mottershead get out until he's over his spite.

It began to appear that his prayers were to be answered as day followed day in an unremarkable round of domestic events. The summer finally drew to a close and the days began to shorten. October first was Dawn's birthday and it had become the custom over the years they had been neighbours for she, Ann, Trevor and Philip to celebrate the event with a night out. This year, for the first time, Ann found herself in need of a baby-sitter.

'It's only the day after tomorrow,' she complained to Philip. 'And I've no idea who to ask.'

'Has Dawn any suggestions?' he tried hopefully.

'Not really. She always gets her mother to come. She did say I could take Melanie across in the carry-cot, but I don't really like to impose.'

'I don't see why not, if she has offered.'

'Yes, but I don't know whether she has asked her mother or not. I mean, it's probably Dawn's idea and her mother is getting rather old to cope with a tiny baby 'specially one that's just been wished on her like that.'

'Well, look,' Philip suggested, 'why don't I ask Helen if she'll come?'

'What, Helen from work, you mean? Does she know anything about looking after infants?'

'Good heavens, Ann. It's only for a couple of hours. Helen's an intelligent girl. I'm sure she'd be quite capable.'

Ann made a determined effort, 'Yes. Yes, of course. Ask her tomorrow then, will you?'

Helen received the request with enthusiasm. 'I'd love to,' she told Philip sincerely. 'You can tell Ann from me that I'm a dab hand with babies.'

Her confident assurance did much to overcome Ann's nervous reluctance at leaving her child and, having once explained to the girl about Melanie's feed, she tucked her hand under Philip's arm and prepared to enjoy her night out.

They were using Trevor's car and, following their regular pattern, were to have a drink at the Austins' before they left for the restaurant. It needed no detective work for them to sense they'd walked in on a domestic squabble as they entered the house. Dawn's cheeks were flushed an angry red, her eyes still held the glitter of suppressed temper and she made little response to their birthday greetings.

Trevor, wearing a hang-dog expression, did his utmost to dissipate the charged atmosphere as he poured their drinks. 'Glad you managed a baby-sitter,' he said brightly to Ann.

'I've been hearing quite a lot about the fabulous Helen just lately, so I thought it about time I made her acquaintance. Just to find out the extent of the competition.' She raised a teasing eyebrow and smiled at her husband as she spoke.

'There you are, you see, Phil. She's not done with you yet.' Dawn's quick response held an underlying edge.

'Take no notice, you two,' Trevor felt obliged to explain. 'We've had a firm offer for the house today, which hasn't pleased Dawn as you may by now have gathered.'

'Oh no!' Ann's cry of dismay was involuntary. 'I was hoping . . .' She let her sentence go unfinished as she realized the danger of appearing to take sides.

'Yes. Well, you weren't hoping any stronger than I was.' Dawn pounced on the opportunity to air her views. 'It's nothing short of ridiculous, selling this place. Especially when you see where he wants us to live.' A footstep creaked the floorboards above and Dawn jerked her thumb at the ceiling. 'I daren't even tell her!'

'I don't see what it has to do with your mother where we live, Dawn.' The conversational manner of Trevor's reply did nothing to stem his wife's temper.

'Oh, *don't* you? Well let me just ask who you think has been looking after the kids every time we've wanted to go out. Who has been close enough for me to call on whenever I've needed her? My mother. That's who. And now you want us to move miles and miles away.'

'It isn't miles away. It's just out the other side of town.'

'Yes, *that* side. The side farthest away. The snob area.'

'Don't talk so silly. The King's Park estate is no more snobby than this. And anyway we're supposed to be celebrating tonight, so let's forget about it for now.'

'You can forget if you like but I'm warning you,

Trevor. I shan't sit tamely aside and let you play ducks and drakes with my life. Sheer cowardice, that's all it is. You've let that half-witted scum scare you into running.' Dawn flung out of the room and her footsteps could be heard pounding up the stairs.

'I'm sorry.' Trevor apologized. 'I'll give her a few minutes to cool down, then I'll go up . . . I . . . Perhaps you'd rather we called tonight off?'

Philip looked towards Ann for her answer and she, feeling Trevor's deep embarrassment, wondered how best to reply. She was saved from making any answer as Dawn's mother called to them. 'Dawn's just putting her lipstick on, she won't keep you a minute. Though why she needs any paint with the colour she's got tonight I'll never know,' she finished as she entered the room. 'Oh, hello, Ann. How are you? And how's that baby? Ah, here's the birthday girl.'

Dawn followed her mother into the room, the flush of temper still in her cheeks but dressed nevertheless for out-doors in the new coat that had been Trevor's birthday gift to her. Nevertheless, the evening was doomed, and the four friends eventually returned home to part on a rather strained note.

Feeling it best to allow them time to work on their problems, Philip avoided contact with Dawn and Trevor over the next few days but Ann reported to him that the relationship between the couple had now deteriorated to the point of open hostility. Their removal date was fixed for the twentieth, the new tenants being due to move in the following day, and Dawn steadfastly refused to make any effort to get the new home ready. Ann was concerned about the effect this state of affairs was having on Mark and David.

'They're becoming afraid. They seem to think they are going to be dragged off to some terrible place,' she told

Philip. 'They are very upset about the move. I've tried to make Dawn see that she is being unfair but she just doesn't seem to care.'

'Could be that it's Trevor who is being unfair,' Philip said briefly.

'You can't really believe that.' Ann was indignant. 'After all, he's only doing what he sees as best for them all.'

'And Dawn won't accept that he is right. I'm not so sure that he is either.'

Ann thought this over. 'Then you wouldn't be prepared for us to move? Not even for Melanie Jane's sake?' she asked carefully.

'That doesn't come into it. What I am saying is that Trevor is forcing his wife and kids into a move none of them wants. And all for what?'

'For peace of mind, surely. He's looking to keep them away from the sort of trouble there has been around here.'

'But it's over now, isn't it? So what's the point in their moving?' he asked crossly.

'If it's over, then why do you still look over your shoulder on dark nights?' Ann asked quietly.

Knowing himself to be bested, Philip took refuge in noisily flapping open the evening paper and retired to sulk behind it. The evening following this conversation, in an effort to heal the breach between his two friends, and partly to regain his place in Ann's good books, he took himself over the road with the proposal that the Butlers should join the Austins in a Saturday picnic at the new house. It was standing empty waiting to be measured and taped, scoured and scrubbed, preparatory to receiving its new occupants. Why didn't they all go together, get all the bits and pieces that needed attention over between them, and make a social outing of it into the bargain.

'After all,' he said, warming to his theme. 'Ann and I

haven't had the opportunity to view the place yet. It will give you a chance to show it off to us.'

Trevor flashed him a grateful glance. 'That's a great idea, Phil. What do you say, Dawn?' he asked.

Dawn was not to be placated so easily. 'If you like.' She shrugged negligently and turned her attention back to the television set.

'What about you two?' Philip addressed David and Mark who were sprawled on the floor playing some make-believe space game. Mark pretended not to have heard and embarked on a noisy flight from Earth to Mars which Philip calculated to be a deliberate attempt to divert his question. 'Hey! Hey, listen to me. Pay attention or I'll call in the inter-galactic probe missiles and have you earth-lings annihilated.' His ploy succeeded in gaining their wary attention and he followed through quickly with, 'Aunty Ann and I want you to show us round that super new house of yours. We've heard it faces just the right direction for spotting UFOs. Now how about that?'

'Oh, Uncle Philip, you are silly.' David forgot his nervous prejudice as Philip continued to tease, and he was gratified to have gained both childrens' promise to give him a complete and guided tour of the house and its locality before he wished them good night.

Dawn glared at him as she led the two boys towards the stairs, her manner that of one feeling betrayed. Philip lowered his glance, a little ashamed at having failed to back her in what he felt in his heart of hearts to be a justified objection.

'I'm glad you came over, Phil. I'm sure Dawn will come round once she sees we all feel the same way about this move.' Trevor was pathetically grateful to have won his support.

Philip felt double the traitor as he murmured, 'Ye-es, well, can't have you two at each other's throats now, can we?'

Dawn took advantage of the visit to the new house to have a private word with Philip. Ann had taken the two boys along to the small shopping precinct adjoining the estate, leaving Trevor and Melanie Jane in sole occupation of the fitted kitchen while she and Philip toured the upper floor. 'What do you think?' She slouched against the door of the boys' proposed bedroom and studied Philip, who made a show of looking about him.

'It's not bad. Not bad at all. You'll have more room here, won't you, than you have at Lynden Grove.'

'Oh come on, Phil. You know I'm not on about the wretched house. I want to know what you think about Trevor dragging us all over here.'

'W-e-ll, it's not all that far away, Dawn. And . . . And I suppose . . .' He grimaced, at a loss to know how to continue.

'And you suppose we'll all live happily ever after. Is that it? Then you've got another think coming,' Dawn said through clenched teeth. 'I thought I could rely on you to support me but I see you're as bad as he is.' She stabbed angrily down at the floor with her thumb. 'All mouth and trousers, you men, when it comes to the crunch.'

'Now, Dawn, be fair. What do you expect me to say? Tie yourself to the stair-rail? Refuse to be moved? Chuck him out? It's not on, you know.' He ran a hand distractedly through his hair. 'As it happens I . . . I think Trevor has been just a shade hasty, but . . . I . . . Oh hell, Dawn, I don't want to quarrel with either of you.' He crossed to her side and placing his hands on her shoulders turned her to face him. 'We shall miss you. You've been wonderful neighbours to Ann and me, but we can still go on being friends, can't we?'

Dawn swayed towards him. 'You know we can, Philip. It isn't that I'm so angry about. I simply object to being driven out of my home by a bunch of mindless morons. I feel we should do as you are doing — stay on and fight back.'

'Well, all the fighting's over now, thank the Lord. So why not forget it?' Philip spoke softly, giving her shoulders an encouraging squeeze.

As he did so, Trevor's head appeared over the top of the banister. He stared at them silently for a brief second. 'I came to tell you coffee is ready,' he said, his voice booming from the bare walls and causing the embracing couple to start guiltily.

'Oh good. And not before time,' Philip replied, his attempt at humour ringing oddly false in the face of Trevor's questioning glance.

Despite the faint air of constraint that developed between the two men, it appeared the day had been a success in so far as it saw the two Austin children more ready to accept their change of address and a certain softening in Dawn's attitude to the pending move. Consequently when October 20th dawned, a bright autumn day holding the warmth of the dying summer in its sunfilled hours, there was an almost festive air about the activities at No. 11, Lynden Grove. Ann put Melanie Jane down for her nap and went across to lend a hand with the packing as did most of their neighbours. Dawn directed operations with a return of her usual efficient vigour, and on the whole the removal of the Austin family was accomplished in a delightfully light-hearted manner.

The release of tension acted like a tonic on Ann, mitigating her initial sense of loss and carrying her happily through the last fine days of October into the misty shortening light of early November. Unpredictable as ever, the good weather went on, the morning mists lifting from the grass to bring days filled with the scent of woodsmoke and chrys-anthemums, and warm afternoon sunshine. On one such sparkling day Ann, returning from a shopping expedition, wheeled the pram into the drive, lugged it indoors over the high front doorstep, and parked it with its slumbering occupant in its customary place alongside Philip's proudly constructed half-wall. She unclipped the shopping-bag and stole a peep at the baby, deciding against lifting her out until she had taken in the lineful of nappies drying in the back garden. It would be dark soon, the day was already dampening down, and she was hopeful of getting them in and folded before Melanie wakened to demand her attention.

Humming a light-hearted if somewhat tuneless little ditty, she was starting back towards the house with the laden wash-basket on her hip when she heard the first screams. She threw the basket from her, heedlessly scattering the clean linen on the damp earth as she fled up the garden path. Further screams, anguished, crucified, leaped out at her as she gained the kitchen door and blundered through towards the hall, illuminated now by sharp, spitting sparks. The flame at their core was centred on her baby's pram.

'NO-OOO!' With a hoarse cry that refuted the horror before her Ann flung herself forwards, her outstretched fingers grasping, grabbing, inches short of the spewing flames. Even as she fell the sound of the explosion jerked her back to her feet and she staggered in drunken dis-orientation until her fingers found and gripped the side of the pram. Pulling it over, spilling the smouldering covering in a heap, she snatched the limp little body into her arms. Dropping to her knees, she cradled the lifeless form to her breast, rocking backwards and forwards, an unearthly keening breaking from her lips.

How long she knelt there, how much precious time she wasted, Ann was never to know. So close was she to the abyss of permanent darkness that she might have re-mained there forever had not the dimpled little hand, wet with the rain of her tears, clenched suddenly and convulsively against her cheek.

She felt the slight movement through a shrouding fog of disbelief. Her heart lurched, jumped and finally burst into a flood of scalding relief as her senses told her she had not been misled. 'Melanie! Melanie! Oh, my baby, my darling, my little love.' Babbling uncontrollably, she lurched to her feet, the precious burden held tight in her arms. Without knowing what she did, she let herself out of the front door and ran headlong and blindly down the front drive, across the road and up the drive of the house opposite. 'Help me! Help me.' She pounded the door with her knees and feet, refusing even for one moment to release her grip on the child. 'He-elp, Dawn. Help me!'

'Ann! For God's sake! Whatever is the matter?' Sue Turner had witnessed the frantic migration from the house next door and had waited only to hear Ann call out before she had followed across the road in her wake.

'Help us, oh please, help us.' The plea came in a piteous whisper, the face Ann turned toward her neighbour almost past recognition in her desperation.

Sue stared at her aghast as a host of fearful possibilities, each more dreadful than the last, crowded in on her shocked mind. She knew full well, as did most of their neighbours how ill Ann had been. Was this an eruption of a badly disturbed mind? And the baby? . . . What had Ann done?

In trepidation Sue tore her gaze from that blanched countenance and lowered her eyes to the bundle locked against her neighbour's chest. There was a crimson stain creeping between the fingers spread protectively against the child's bonneted head.

'Ann?' Sue's voice pitched at an unattainable octave cracked the name as a question.

'The hospital . . . Get us there.'

The burning eyes locked on to hers, lending strength to her suddenly shaking limbs as she braced herself to act.

'Come with me.' Turning Ann about, she led her swiftly back over the road and through her own open front door. The overturned pram and still smouldering blankets blocked Sue's path for only a second. With the strength of desperation she flung all aside and snatched up the telephone. Her eyes fixed on the woman turned zombie, she attempted to dial. Fingers over-anxious and clumsy fumbled their way round the three nines.

Answer! Oh God, why didn't they answer? The steady purrr, purrr mocked her desperate haste. At last the metallic-voiced query, then she was gabbling her frantic request.

No words were exchanged after that phone call, no move broke their paralysed stance. Two pairs of eyes gazed unblinkingly into each other as they waited and listened for the siren that would release them from this terrible spell.

CHAPTER 12

Waiting . . . Waiting . . . Waiting. Locked into a never-ending green-walled vacuum, each surging beat of her heart recording a lifetime caught on this treadmill, Ann sat immobile. Wave after wave of choking prayer emanated from the core of her being to swell and expand, beating against the suffocating walls of the small hospital waiting-room, coming back at her, heavy, syrupy, drowning her in their cloying embrace.

Let her be all right . . . let her be all right . . . let her be all right. Over and over, on and on. Would that door never open? Her eyes flicked towards the cream-painted panels, the only movement she had made since becoming a part of the tubular metal and canvas the hospital described as a chair.

Outside, beyond that impersonal woodwork — footsteps, rubber-soled, hurrying. A swish of starched skirts, the sigh of a closing door. Somewhere a voice, laughter-filled, uncaring — part of that other world. Back to the importuning plea: Let her be all right . . . let her . . . let her . . .

Footsteps, a double set, fast approaching the door. Ann shrank imperceptibly, shielding the raw open wound that was herself from further hurt. The toe of a shoe striking against the weighty door rang woodenly, bringing a gasp from her lips as it opened too slowly to admit the hurrying man.

'Philip!' For a moment neither of them moved, then with a cry Ann flung herself into his arms. 'Philip, Philip. It's her face, her face.' A violent tremor shook her from head to toe and Philip fought to hold her erect. The nurse, appearing from behind his left shoulder took a professional assessment and stepped quickly back through the doorway. It seemed only seconds before she came back carrying a covered tray.

'Get her coat off,' she ordered Philip. 'And roll up her sleeve.' She plunged the needle into a corked bottle, tipping it upright she drew back the plunger. 'There.' The injection over, she swabbed the puncture in Ann's upper arm with a cotton-wool swab. 'You'll soon feel better now,' she said sympathetically. And indeed the violent shudders were already giving way to a more controlled shivering. Lifting Ann's coat from the floor, she placed it about her shoulders and pressed her back into the chair. 'Sit quietly for a moment or two. I'll get someone to bring you a nice cup of tea.' She straightened and turned to Philip. 'You'll be all right?' she asked, her face anxious.

He nodded, his lips compressed into a thin line.

She studied him for a moment or two, then, apparently satisfied, she scooped up the tray and swept out of the room.

Philip stared down at the hunched shoulders. The draped

coat seemed over-large for Ann's slight figure and rucked about her slender neck before flaring grotesquely where the shoulder-pads stood high and empty. He reached out a comforting hand, was lost as to where he might touch, and his fingers splayed uselessly above the bent head before he let his arm drop to his side. Hooking his toe behind the tubular steel of the chair to his right, he dragged it forward until it stood beneath his hand. Metal clanged as he placed it closely alongside Ann's and he clenched his teeth with a grimace at the noise in this cushioned atmosphere.

Seating himself, he reached to take both Ann's cold hands into his own. They didn't speak. There were no words. An orderly brought tea with a murmured excuse for disturbing their vigil. She left without their ever being aware of her fleeting visit. The watch on Philip's wrist pecked away at the seconds with an abnormally loud tick. They waited.

The door opened bringing a surgeon, white-gowned and grim-faced, into the room. Philip rose swiftly, the metal chairlegs scraping. Ann started, then tightened her tenacious grip on his right hand.

A ward sister accompanied the man. 'This is Mr and Mrs Butler,' she explained unnecessarily before stepping to one side.

'Ah, yes . . . Wouldn't you rather be seated?' he asked. His careful, low-pitched voice brought the world back with a rush and the normal everyday sounds tumbled into the room, pushing away its cloistered padding.

Philip shook his head slowly, reaching down in response to the insistent tug on his arm to help Ann to her feet.

The surgeon stood silent, probing them with his eyes, gauging their likely reaction to the news he must break.

The tension mounted until it seemed to Philip that he could endure it no longer and would throw himself at the man, beat at him insanely until he managed to drag out of him all there was to be told.

'I'm sorry . . . It's not good.' The man's whole demeanour conveyed his sympathy. Philip braced himself and tightened his arm about Ann's shoulders. 'There is extensive damage to the left side of the head and face. The eye . . . Her hearing . . . There is some brain damage . . . Impossible to say how much at this stage . . . She is a very, very sick little girl. Perhaps . . .' He flapped his arms expressively.

'No!' The word was clipped and precise. 'No, it would *not* be best if she died.'

Philip stared amazed at the virago who thrust herself upright away from his supportive embrace.

Ann's face registered a fierce determination. 'She is going to get better. I know it. She can have surgery— they do wonderful things—wonderful.' She collapsed so suddenly neither the two men nor the sister was able to prevent her falling to the floor.

'It's the shock, Mr Butler, coupled with the effects of the injection. She'll come to in a moment.' The sister checked Ann's pulse, a low groan from her patient confirming her prediction. 'Oh, she seems to have burned herself.' Capable fingers moved down from the wrist to unclench the relaxed fist. 'H,mm, that needs a dressing.'

'N-nothing . . . It's . . . not . . . not . . .'

'Shh, don't try to talk. Take a deep breath. That's right . . . Now out . . . And again . . . Lovely . . . Now out . . . That's a good girl.' A touch of colour returned to the corpse-white cheeks as Ann meekly obeyed.

'There. Feeling better now, are we? Come along then, my dear, sit up and let me take another look at that hand.'

Ann raised her hand to her face and stared at it stupidly. Her uninjured right hand reached out to paw at the blackened flesh and blisters in the palm before dabbing along the swollen fingers as though discovering their existence for the first time. Letting both hands fall, she pushed herself upright, her eyes searching for Philip. 'We should have moved,' she said distinctly. 'Like Trevor and Dawn. They couldn't have hurt her if we'd only moved.'

They remained all night at the hospital. Arrangements were made for Ann to have the use of a bed in a room close to the intensive care unit, but she was unable to rest and insisted on joining Philip in the now familiar waiting-room. There was nothing either of them could do to help Melanie Jane, they were painfully aware of that, but neither could they submit to the doctor's instruction to get whatever rest they were able.

Being there, close at hand, awake and steeled to meet any change in their baby's condition allowed them to feel just that one degree less incapable. So they stayed, gravel-eyed and sleepless, in the green-and-cream-painted prison. They talked at first, over the innumerable cups of hospital tea, about how they would raise the funds to buy the best possible care for their child, about how they would love her, cherish her, and make up to her somehow for all the pain she must now endure. They told each other earnestly about the fantastic strides the medical profession was making, about how advanced the techniques were in plastic surgery, how it was early days yet and things might not be as bad as they seemed. And they knew, each of them, in the chill core of their hearts that their child was irreversibly damaged. The talk petered out, the silence closed in, beyond the cream-painted door an occasional sound, muffled and stealthy, spoke of the constant vigil kept over the suffering and the sick.

'Why don't you go and lie down, love?' Philip's voice rasped, betraying his own weariness as he took his wife's hand.'

She shook her head mutely.

'Come on, don't make yourself ill too.'

'I'm all right! Leave me alone,' Ann snapped at him, snatching her hand away. 'You go home if you want to.'

'Not until I know you are getting some rest.'

'Then we will both stay where we are.'

And so they sat on, sounds of increased activity telling them when the hospital day was beginning, the bustle and movement outside their forgotten domain reminding them of things to be done.

'Will you go in to work?' Ann asked, her grey face lacking any spark of interest.

'Probably. Just to let them know. I won't stay though.'

'If you're going near home, could you bring me some things in?'

'Of course I'm going near home. Where else would I go?' Philip bit back the tetchy anger induced by the long sleepless night. 'And I'll bring you anything you need, you know that,' he added more gently.

'I'd better give you a list, I suppose . . . I . . .' For a moment he thought she would break down but she bit hard on her lower lip and controlled the threatening tears.

'There's time yet. I'll stay with you a while longer.' He yearned to take her into his arms, to smooth the tumbled dark hair and kiss away the stiff-faced mask she was using to cover her anguish, but her manner warned him to keep his distance and not to intrude. He sighed helplessly and turned to direct his stare out of the window. It was still dark beyond the misted panes and his own reflection was lost in the haze of condensation.

'Go now!'

'What did you say?'

'Go! Go now . . . Go and tell them at work or whatever.' Ann sprang to her feet, her arms hugging her slender body, her back turned determinedly in his direction. Philip opened his mouth to protest, thought better of it, and after a few moments of hesitation walked out leaving her in sole possession of the comfortless room.

Ann maintained her position until she heard the door whisper to a close behind him; then she turned, one hand clenched and pressed against her trembling lips, the other in its protective cocoon of bandages dangling uselessly at her side. Oh God. Why had she done that—spoken to him in that way? Hadn't they enough hurt between them without her making it worse? Sightlessly she lowered her head, bringing her hands together at her waist, her sound hand gripping the other in a punishing hold, twisting, squeezing, pressing at the wound as if by wreaking this torture upon her flesh she could lessen the stabbing pain in her heart.

Philip stumbled across the unlit visitors' car-park, his tired eyes failing to adjust to the darkness after the constant glare of the fluorescent tubes. He unlocked the car and slid across the cold plastic seating behind the steering-wheel. A misting of frost smeared the windscreen and he groped under the dashboard for the aerosol can of de-icer he always carried. The cold metal can stung his palm and he snatched his fingers back sharply from the contact, his brain sending messages of danger along his outstretched arm. His stomach muscles contracted defensively as for one split second he believed himself to be burned. Then the tingling perspiration of relief washed over him as his senses registered his mistake, and on its heels came the full crawling horror of the agony that had been inficted on his defenceless child. He stared straight ahead, seeing that terrible moment re-enacted on the milky-white surface of the windscreen.

They had told him at the hospital that the injuries had been caused by a firework. A banger. The police had been more specific and had described it as one of those extravagantly explosive devices beloved of small boys, known under the trade name of 'Blockbuster'. They had told him also, in answer to his wild instinctive accu-

sations, that yes, Mottershead had been released on conclusion of his sentence. Yes, it had been very recently.

'But I must caution you against making unfounded
accusations in public, Mr Butler,' Sergeant Parker had
warned. 'It's understandable that you are, er, upset . . .'
He had paused considering the inadequacy of the word,
then gone on: 'But there is no evidence, no evidence whatso-
ever, to tie Mottershead in with this thing.'

'He said he would get me. He threatened me in court.
You must be aware of that,' Philip had blazed at him.

'It's not enough, sir. We can't pull him in on the strength
of some half-hysterical threats.'

'Then you'll do nothing? Is that what you are saying?
The way you sat back and did nothing when we were
being driven half crazy by those hell-hounds before?'

Parker made allowances for Philip's distressed condition. 'I believe I explained at the time, I came to the
case late in the game but I had no reason then or now to
believe it was handled inefficiently.' He ignored the
derisive snort that greeted this but his voice took on a
firmer tone. 'We don't live in a police state, Mr Butler. In
this country a man is innocent until proved guilty. And
this applies to your former tormentors. We can't arrest
people for walking the streets. The proper precautions
were taken. Men detailed for night patrols. Lacking proof
of malicious intent, there was nothing more we could do.'

'And now? What about now?' Philip had risen to his
feet wild-eyed and distraught, his gaze beating down on
the sergeant.

'We'll ask the proper questions, sir. In all the right
quarters,' Parker said meaningfully. And Philip had been
obliged to leave it at that.

Half-formed recollections of that conversation persisted,
and the explanation offered of that most terrible event.
The firework, he was told, had been slipped through his
letter-box and had fallen on to the baby sleeping in her

pram just below, lodging somehow inside the rim of her fluffy pink bonnet. In fear and pain the child had screamed and thrashed, trapping the erupting incendiary against the side of her head. So vivid was Philip's vision he found his hands shooting out to snatch her to safety. His knuckles crashing against the ice-encrusted glass brought him back to himself with a jolt. I'll find them. I'll find the bastards responsible if it's the last thing I do, he promised himself, and discovered when he got out of the car to spray the windscreen that his legs were trembling uncontrollably and his fist clenched convulsively about the aerosol tin.

As he drove through the dark morning streets, lights snapped on in the upper rooms of the houses he passed signalling the start of yet another working day. The odd lorry and milk-float travelling his way were joined by a trickle of family cars as he neared the town. Early birds, he thought fleetingly, and pushed the accelerator pedal down; he wanted to be over the other side of this concrete jungle before the real influx of traffic began. He'd have a wash and shave, collect Ann's things from the house — Damn! He'd forgotten to ask what she'd need. His speed eased momentarily as he debated whether to turn about now, go back to the hospital and ask, or to make a calculated guess at the sort of things she'd be wanting. The guess won favour and he continued on his way with a mental picture of his wife's face as he'd last seen it, bone-white and drained, dancing before his eyes. He drove automatically, tracking his route across the still slumbering town by a sort of inbuilt radar. As he approached the main highway the amber warning lights of a pedestrian crossing beamed out at him, calling his wandering thoughts to the task in hand. He began braking even as his gaze fell on the youth starting across the road and the amber light changed to red reflecting the blood spot in his vision as he recognized the studded jacket, the skin-tight blue jeans and the general air of 'bugger you, Jack'. It was Mottershead!

Without conscious thought he gripped the steering-wheel and slammed the accelerator pedal down to the floor.

Rubber burned from the racing rear wheels as the car surged forwards. The impact as it struck Mottershead full on lifted him in a welter of spinning limbs before slamming his body across the car bonnet.

Through the narrow, crazed eyes of revenge Philip gazed his last on the human garbage that had cost him so dear. The bearded jaws were agape in an endless scream of protest, the distended eyes registered tremendous shock, and from the shaven skull the left ear protruded, its golden ornament winking incongruously in the light thrown from the standard at the edge of the crossing.

The body slid from sight and the car hurtled on, a nauseous bump lifting one rear wheel as flesh and bone cracked beneath its punishing weight and Philip fought to control the mad sideways plunge that threatened to overturn him. The spinning wheels regained their purchase and he risked tapping the brakes. In the wing-mirror the dark, huddled pile shrank away behind him until it was nothing more than discarded litter left by chance in the road.

Reaction began to set in. Philip bit back the bile that rose in his throat and tried to concentrate on his next move. He was not going to report the incident; there was nothing more certain than that! An eye for an eye, he told himself grimly as his hands began to shake on the wheel, forcing him to reduce speed even further. He didn't think he had been seen, there were no tell-tale headlights on the road behind him, no pedestrians as yet on the normally thronged pavements, and he had managed to put nearly a mile between himself and the crossing without being challenged. He drove on, carefully now as the enormity of what he had done set his teeth chattering and bathed his body in a cold, clammy sweat.

He couldn't go home, he realized suddenly. Not to an empty house and the self-accusations that would come the minute he began to turn this thing over. No, he couldn't go home . . . So where? The thought of Dawn and her sup-portive condemnation of the scum he'd just hit back at — his mind balked at using the word murdered — drew him like a homing beacon and he took the next turning that would put him in the right direction for her new home. Once on the road there, another, more urgent thought occurred to him and he made a slight detour that would take him out past the old disused freight terminal, where he pulled into the weedy, overgrown ground well clear of the part where any chance passer-by might spot him. He got out of the car and made to step around to the front intending to check on the amount of damage it had sustained, but before he reached the end of the bonnet he felt his legs begin to buckle and he caught at the smooth metal trying to keep himself upright. His fingers rubbed uselessly down the painted surface, he watched them as in a slow-motion film as he slid to his knees. The rush of bile he'd been at pains to fight down rose now like the opened sluice of a dam, and he was left retching and heaving painfully on an empty stomach before the tide passed and he was able to push himself to his feet.

Wiping his streaming eyes on his handkerchief, he re-sumed his intended inspection, swaying a little unsteadily as he took a pace backwards the better to judge the overall state of the car. The front was caved in, the radiator pushed back to the engine, deep scores ran from front to back of the foreshortened bonnet, the number-plate dangled and the off-side headlight pointed upwards at an angle of forty degrees. Philip studied the damage, his fingers reaching out automatically to pluck the fibres of cloth from their anchorage in the twisted metal round the radiator grille. He rolled them absently between his fingers, his mind fumbling and numb, unable to deal with the problem of how to get the car put to rights before anyone should come asking difficult questions. It was a miracle the thing had got him this far in its present state, he decided and he was reluctant to chance taking it back on the road. Not only would it be unsafe, but it was patently obvious from the extent of the damage that it had been involved in a major accident. Brushing the little pill he had kneaded from the cloth fibres from his perspiring fingers, he drew deeply on the frosty air. The effect on his weary, sleep-deprived brain was intoxicating. His head whirled sickeningly and his legs turned to rubber. Suddenly, he felt dreadfully, vulnerably alone. He couldn't deal with this situation without help. Lurching unsteadily, he concentrated all his energies into placing one foot after the other as he set out to walk the remaining distance to the King's Park estate.

The day was beginning in earnest by the time he reached the end of his hike. Cars, emerging backwards from the bowels of integral garages, interrupted the careful rhythm of his pace as he passed down the road. He paused at each such occurrence to watch with dull eyes as loving young husbands raised a hand in farewell salute to their wives watching for this everyday pledge of affection before beginning their rounds of domestic chores. Had there ever been a time when he and Ann had counted themselves part of that weekly ritual, he wondered; the troubled existence had become so much a part of his lot he had forgotten how it was to wish his wife goodbye without adding a fervent prayer that she and their home would be safe until his return. He turned into the open gateway of Dawn's front garden feeling as old as time.

The front door opened at his approach proclaiming that Dawn too had been taking leave of her man, or at least had been watching out of her window in company with her new neighbours.

'Philip! What on earth . . . Why aren't you at the hospital?'

'Hospital?' he stared at her without comprehension. He had become so immersed in the task of just getting to the place where he now stood that he'd lost sight of all that had passed before he began walking.

'Here, come along in.' Dawn drew him into the house and proceeded to guide him through to the sitting-room as though he was blind.

Philip passed a hand wearily over his face as memory returned. 'You've heard then? You know?'

'Yes, I know. Sue Turner rang and told me, and I've been ringing the hospital. I told them I was your sister. I hope you don't mind but they tell you nothing unless they think you're a relative.'

'No, no. I don't mind at all.' He dropped into the nearest chair, glad to be spared the necessity of explaining that much at least.

'So why aren't you with Ann? And what *are* you doing walking out here?' She waited on his reply with a patience wholly foreign to her impetuous nature.

'I've killed him!' The grey eyes met hers squarely, his voice remained expressionless as he made the confession.

'Who, for God's sake? Philip, are you all right?'

He dropped his head into his hands as he began to shake uncontrollably.

She stared at him, appalled. What was happening here? Was this some kind of nightmare? She glanced swiftly around as if to assure herself that this was the same familiar room she'd been standing in only seconds before when she'd watched Trevor start on his way. Her eyes returned to the man crouched in the chair. Had this latest blow been too much?

Even as the thought entered her mind Philip made a

valiant effort to speak. 'I . . . I've killed . . . him. *Him*, *Mottershead*.' He forced the words between his clenched teeth.

Dawn groped weakly behind her for some means of support as she took in the full horror of what he was saying. Her fingers found and gripped the edge of the door, she braced her spine along its narrow width, feeling the metal latch bite into the muscles of her back. It was some time before she could bring herself to ask, 'H—how?'

'I ran him down. In the car. I was . . . He was . . . I've killed him, I tell you. That enough, isn't it? He asked for it. He deserved it!' Anger was coming to Philip's aid now, lending him the strength to quell his nervous shaking. He raised his head and stared at her. 'He mutilated my child . . . He's not fit to live.'

'But how did you know where to find him? . . . I thought he went to prison or some such.' Dawn was recovering rapidly from the shock of Philip's revelation.

'So he did. But you know how it is these days. They only lock them up as a gesture, they're back on the streets inside a month to commit the same bloody crimes all over again.'

'Well, he's one that won't, at least.' Dawn dismissed Mottershead and her last remaining qualms in the same breath. She studied Philip, a new light in her eyes. 'When did it happen? I mean, how? Where?'

'When did I run him over? An hour ago, maybe two. I was on my way home . . . I have to do something about the car, Dawn.' He was suddenly brought to the reason for his visit.

'Where is it?'

'On that waste ground out by the old freight terminal. It's in a bit of a mess.' He began to pick nervously at the braid on the arm of his chair.

Dawn noticed the action and immediately took charge. 'Look, come into the kitchen away from these windows.'

She jerked her head at the expanse of glass. 'All the estate knows your business in these aquariums,' she added wryly.

'Where are the boys?' Philip asked as he followed her from the room.

'Mark's at school, Trevor takes him on his way in to work. And David is up in his room.'

'He's very quiet.'

'He's learning sense! I've walloped him once already today. He's keeping out of my way now.' The tone of her voice invited no comment and Philip was too deeply involved in his own affairs to sit in judgement. 'Now then, sit down at the table and I'll make us a coffee. Like something to eat?'

'Er, no. No, thanks, Dawn.'

'Right then, won't be a jiffy . . . There!' It seemed only seconds before she was placing two steaming mugs on the table. 'I'm having whisky in mine, I think you had better do the same,' she advised. Giving him no chance to refuse, she tipped the bottle generously over his cup.

Philip sipped the scalding liquid, feeling some of the tension drain out of him as the fiery spirit hit his stomach.

'Now tell me all about it,' Dawn invited.

He began a wooden recital.

'I — er — I don't suppose you know anybody that would fix the car for me?' he finished without a great deal of hope.

'Why have it fixed?'

'You should see it, Dawn. I can't drive it around in its present state, apart from its not being roadworthy everybody would know . . . They're going to come looking for me once they identify Mottershead in any case.'

'Not necessarily, and you misunderstand me. What I meant was, why don't you leave it where it is and simply report it stolen?'

'I can't do that! Think of all the questions . . . The

police . . . What would I say?' But the idea was growing in its appeal and he voiced his protests without a great deal of conviction.

'No need to say very much at all. Just go back to the hospital and make like you've only just missed it. That way you'll give yourself an alibi for the time of . . . of the, er . . . the accident.'

'It wouldn't work. Ann will know what time I left. If I go back now and say the car's been stolen she's going to want to know what I've been doing in the meantime.'

'Well, can't you tell her? Get her to back you up? After all, Melanie is her baby too, and it was because of—'

'Don't, Dawn.' Philip's voice was sharp. 'Don't, please, ever lay the blame for what I've just done on that baby's head.'

'I didn't mean it like that . . . I just meant . . .' She shrugged dismissively. 'Anyway Ann will want to help, won't she?'

'I . . . No, no, I daren't risk telling her,' Philip admitted after much thought.

'Then we'll think of another way.' Dawn closed ranks against the absent woman, dismissing any viewpoint that wasn't directly helpful as useless. 'It's like I keep telling Trevor, You've got to look out for number one in this world or go under. And I'm glad someone has had the guts to do something back at those evil sods.' She reached across the table and gave his hand an encouraging squeeze.

Philip lifted his coffee mug and frowned at the dregs lying in the bottom. Inspiration rose from the depths. 'I think I know how to do it,' he said slowly. 'Listen to this and tell me what you think. What if I can get home now, without being seen? If I take a leaf out of our ex-tormentor's book and cross over the fields at the back of my place? I can get into the garden through the hedge and into the house the back way without anyone being any the wiser.'

'What good would that do?'

'Well, don't you see? I could claim that I'd been home for ages, that I'd left the car at the hospital because . . . well, because I'd been feeling too bushed to drive. Then I —'

'Then you could call the police from the hospital later! Yes, Philip, yes! I think that's a fantastic idea.' Her enthusiasm shone from her face, warming him, giving him the confidence he had subconsciously been seeking when he'd made the turning that would bring him out here.

'Bless you, Dawn. You're an angel,' he said, reaching over the table to brush her cheek with his lips.

Neither of them saw or heard the small figure of Dawn's youngest son, his round eyes watching this affectionate salute before he crept stealthily back up the stairs to his room.

CHAPTER 13

To enter one's own home clandestinely is much easier said than done, Philip decided as he rounded the corner of the road that would bring him on to the lane crossing the end of Lynden Grove. In spite of his having alighted two stops before his own as an extra precaution, he'd been feeling as conspicuous as a fur coat in a nudist camp ever since he'd left the bus. He had forced himself to walk at a steady pace along the roundabout route he'd taken through the estate, knowing that a hurrying figure would draw curious eyes, but he could feel his face burning with the embarrassment of his own existence as he strode along.

So far he'd been lucky. He'd seen no one he knew on his way over here; all that remained was to get himself across the fields at the rear of Lynden Grove and from there into his own garden. Taking a careful look up and down the lane, he satisfied himself that all was clear before stepping off its gravelled surface to melt from sight among the leafless bushes and trees that formed its boundary. From this vantage point he could see all the rear gardens along the row, including his own. Again luck was with him, for the cold weather had kept most of the children not yet of school age indoors, and providing he kept below the level of the hedge he thought he could manage to reach home without being seen.

Feeling already like a hunted criminal, he began worming his way along the hedgerow. One or two of his neighbours had clipped the rampant hawthorn low enough to conform with their tidy ideas of the conventional hedge and when he reached these he had to drop to his hands and knees to maintain his cover. In spite of the frozen state of the ground he was sweating by the time he reached the point where his own garden ran down to the field. Thankful now that he'd never been tempted to shave his stretch of the hedge, he pushed his way in among the sooty, spine-covered bushes and was about to step out on to his lawn when he heard the Turners' back door being opened. A burst of music swelled briefly before it closed again to cut off the sound.

Philip forced his way back into the hedge, ignoring the pricks and jabs of the hawthorn spikes as he saw Sue, a loaded washing basket in her arms, step around the rear of her house. Lowering the basket to the ground, she took a folded washing-line from the crook of her arm, hooked it to a line-post standing close to the house and began paying it out as she paced her way backwards down the garden path. Fresh perspiration pricked along Philip's flesh as she approached the bottom of the garden and the second post, but she was concentrating exclusively on pegging out the damp washing and unless he made a rash move there was no reason why she should turn and see him. It took her forever to empty the basket. By the time she reached the point where the clothes-line ran nearest to Philip's hiding-place he was feeling racked. A burning pain of tension and strain ran up his right leg and scorched across the small of his back, a particularly spiteful thorn had embedded itself in his left cheek, and his arms throbbed with the agony of trying to keep the wiry branches bent low enough to give him cover while at the same time preventing their clatter and shake as the cold set him shivering.

At last Sue was finished and she started back up the garden flicking the odd garment into shape as she passed. Philip stayed put until he felt absolutely sure she would not be coming back, then he crawled from his hiding-place and, keeping close to the low fence separating the two gardens, wormed his way over lawn and flower-border to his own back door. With fingers stiff and clumsy with cold, he groped through his pockets and fished out his key, then gave a heartfelt sigh of relief as the door yielded under his touch and he stumbled over the threshold into the welcoming warmth of the kitchen.

For a moment he could do no more than stand, his back pressed against the door, giving thanks for his unremarked arrival. A hot bath restored his circulation and did much to relax his tense muscles but he was far too keyed-up to attempt any sleep. Instead, he made a large pot of coffee, cut himself a plate of sandwiches and prepared to work his way through both while he gave further thought to the details of the story he intended to spin. He drank the coffee at a temperature only slightly less than scalding, but the food turned to sawdust in his mouth and his throat closed convulsively, refusing to swallow the nourishment that would have helped give him strength.

Pushing the plate away in disgust, he gave way to the hovering pangs of remorse. There was no doubt in his mind that Mottershead was deserving of punishment, but only now did he question his right to appoint himself executioner. Maybe he should have left well alone — gone to the police and told them of his suspicions, left them to handle the task of meting out just retribution. Crushing back these thoughts as useless and unproductive, he tried again to concentrate on his story. It would help nobody, least of all him, to confess to his crime. What he needed to do now was build up his alibi.

It was to this end that he made as much display of letting himself out of his front door as was likely to seem natural. He wanted the neighbours to see him now, to assume since he was leaving the house that he had been inside for some time. It wasn't until he reached the front gates and was about to step off down the road that it occurred to him he could help things along just a little without it becoming too obvious. Accordingly, he turned into the next drive and went deliberately to seek out the attention of the young woman he'd previously been at such pains to avoid.

Sue Turner answered his knock, her expression of enquiry swiftly turning to one of sympathy as she recognized her caller. 'Hello, Phil. How are things? Is the baby all right? How's Ann? Won't you come in?' Anxious to help in any way she could, the questions poured past her lips.

'Thanks, Sue. No, I won't stay. I . . . I just wanted to ask if you could give me a bit of advice. You see, Ann is staying at the hospital and she wanted me to take her some things . . . clothing and that. Only, I came away without asking what she would need. Would you have any idea? I could ring the hospital, of course, but she might be sleeping and I'd hate them to wake her.'

'Oh, that's easy enough, Phil. She'll want toiletries, soap, toothpaste, stuff like that. And a change of undies I would think, and — Look, why don't I come round with you and put some things together?'

'Would you? That's very kind.' Philip began to feel like a hypocrite but the charade had to be played, so he added, 'I'm afraid I was half asleep when I came home. I should have asked Ann to make me a list, then I needn't have put you to any trouble.'

'It's no trouble. No trouble at all. I'll just tell Mum where I'm going.' Sue disappeared into the house and he heard the murmur of voices as she spoke to someone in the kitchen. She was gone for less than a minute and returned to say briskly, 'Sorry about that, but today is Mum's visiting day and I didn't like to dash off and leave her wondering where I'd gone. Now let's get those things sorted out, shall we?'

They started along Sue's drive together and were met at the gate by June Simpson, the Butlers' neighbour on the other side of the house. By the time he'd given June the latest bulletin on Ann and the baby and, in response to her questions, had explained that he had come home alone in the small hours, leaving Ann at the hospital, Philip felt his alibi to be nicely established.

'I wondered why I'd not seen you come home,' said Sue in conversational tones as he led the way into the house. 'But that explains it. I'm never up much before eight, George is the only early bird in our house.'

'Oh, it was long before eight, there were no lights on in your place when I passed.' Having pressed the point home, Philip judged it was now time to change the subject and was grateful when Sue responded to his introducing the problem of whether he should take Ann a clean dress or a much heavier skirt and sweater.

Not until they had all Sue had collected neatly packed into a suitcase did he realize that here again fate was giving him another perfect opportunity to cover his tracks. He lifted the case experimentally as if testing its weight, assumed a doubtful expression, then said blandly, 'I think we'd better make that the lot, Sue. I've got to take this in by hand, plus all my stuff for the office. I left the car at the hospital, you see.'

'Did you? Whatever for?'

'Too tired to drive. I couldn't even think straight, as you may have guessed, or I'd have known I'd be needing it. Still, it's only for once.' He managed a rueful smile that wasn't entirely false since it held a certain mocking acknowledgement that he had now crossed all the bounds of decency by lying to his friends and making use of them in this way, for Sue would surely pass on all he'd said to her mother and George. Her murmured expressions of sympathy served to heap burning coals on the slow fire of his self-castigation.

Travelling in to work on the bus, he began to wonder whether he would be able to go through with the deceit; only when he thought of the grim alternative did his resolve stiffen. There was no way he was going to prison as a reward for ridding the world of an abomination like Mottershead. This righteous frame of mind carried him into his chief's office and allowed him to accept the older man's expressions of sympathy regarding Melanie Jane and nod in agreement of his expressed hope that the criminals responsible for her injuries might soon be brought to swift and terrible justice.

Escaping at last from the awkwardness of this situation, Philip made straight for Helen Broadhurst's desk. Here was someone he could confide in, someone who would understand without the need for lies and deceit. He could tell it all to Helen, she would need no explanation of the impassioned act of revenge, hadn't she stormed and raged often enough over the passive role he'd been obliged to play? He was almost on the point of confession when it occurred to him that he had no right to unburden himself at Helen's expense. She was a young girl, too young and too impressionable to be crushed under the weight of his guilt. There could be no easing of his troubled conscience in that direction, he decided reluctantly. This was one load he would need to carry alone.

Accepting Helen's genuine compassion was the most difficult exercise he had yet undertaken, the knowledge of his guilt setting him coldly outside the warm circle of her kindly concern. Her heated condemnation of the party responsible for the dreadful act echoed the feelings in his own heart and when the small fist thumped her desk and she raged with tears in her eyes that 'such vile, godless creatures had no right to be born,' his feelings were mirrored exactly. But, a small inner voice asked, was he any better than the hoodlums they were both at such pains to condemn? Hadn't he just committed an act as despicable as that which had injured his daughter? No! he told himself fiercely. No, never that. Melanie Jane was a baby — innocent, pure — while Mottershead . . . Well, he'd asked for his right enough.

'How is Ann taking it?' Helen's question, softly voiced, penetrated his angry thoughts.

He sighed. 'I don't really know. She's badly shocked, of course . . . And deeply distressed, but I don't really know how much she is affected. She's putting up a remarkably good front considering.'

Helen nodded, accepting the helpless lift of his shoulders as the unspoken conclusion of his reply. 'Can I help at all?' she offered. 'I know it sounds trite but if there is anything, cook your meals, bit of washing . . . Anything . . .'

Philip shook his head. 'No, no, thanks, Helen. It's very good of you but . . .' Again the temptation to pour out the whole story was paramount but he choked back the words and substituted, 'Perhaps . . . perhaps later . . . eh?'

'Sure.' She gave him an understanding smile. 'Later.'

*

Lying to Ann was made easy for him by her preoccupation with their baby's condition, which did not appear to have changed significantly since Philip had left. He found her sitting by the side of the glass-sided cot apparently unaware that he had been absent for she gave him no greeting as he walked in, neither did she look up when he placed a comforting hand on her shoulder. He found himself unable to look at the tubes and pipes and wires and pads that snaked their way up from the tiny bandaged form to the complicated machinery that was helping to sustain his daughter's life.

'I've brought your things,' he said in a whisper, lifting the case so that Ann might see. She stared at it incuriously before lowering her eyes back to the cot. Philip looked around for somewhere he might place it out of the way and was forced in the end to ask the aid of one of the nurses who seemed to be in constant occupation of this highly specialized place.

'I'll take it through to Mrs Butler's room,' she offered.

'I'll carry it, you lead the way.' He deposited the case on the bed in the tiny curtained-off cubicle that had been allocated for Ann's use, and detained the nurse when she would have hurried away. 'Just a minute, please. I . . . Can you tell me what will happen now? I mean . . . do we just wait . . . or . . .'

'We wait, I'm afraid, Mr. Butler. We wait for the baby to gain strength. She's comatose at present . . . She may come out of that in a few days—'

'A few days? Do you mean she—'

'There is some brain damage, you know,' the nurse interrupted his startled exclamation, but not unkindly. 'These things take time. When she is stronger, there will be operations, some skin grafts, maybe.'

'Skin grafts? Then you think . . . She *is* going to get better?'

'We must always hope so,' came the non-committal reply before the nurse bustled away to attend to her duties.

Philip trailed reluctantly back to the ward and took a chair by Ann's side. He forced himself to be seated, to assume some semblance of patience, but he burned to be on the move, he was doing no good here. He just couldn't sit and watch the unrecognizable scrap of humanity lying so still, swathed in her bandages, and he marvelled that Ann was able to do so. He stole a sideways glance at his wife. Her face was set and white betraying no emotion; only her hands, the slender fingers of the right hand clutching desperately at the wad of bandages on her left as they lay together in her lap, gave any indication of the tension she was under. When he tried to take that childlike little hand into his own she resisted his touch with all the strength in her fingers and only when he would have withdrawn with muttered impatience did he realize that through the strength of those clasped hands Ann was pouring all her strength into their child, willing her to live with a single-mindedness that left him cut off from any comfort he and Ann might have had of each other. Sitting there, in the hushed atmosphere that seemed to belong as of right to this place, he felt the barriers rising between them. Here he was, offering whatever strength he possessed to lift and sustain her, and she was silently rejecting him. Had she but once looked his way or stretched out her hand to include him in this fight she was waging, they could have gone forward together. But she made no such move and Philip watched all they had turn to dust around the pulsing, dripping tubes feeding life to their child.

The interminable day wore on. Philip dozed a little propped on the hard hospital chair, the strain of his sleepless night overcoming his sense of loss and frustration. As the last of the daylight crept from the sky he roused himself to the point of making fresh plans; he must find some excuse to report his car stolen. If he left it too long he would lose all the advantage of the scheme. Glancing across at Ann, he toyed for one fleeting second with telling her all, with throwing himself at her feet, with begging her for help, for a small part of that love and understanding they had used to share. Oh, the joy and relief of being able to take her into his confidence, knowing her love for him would allow her to understand and forgive. He pushed the idea away even as it was conceived and took up the lonely burden of lies and deceit as he made great show of rising and stretching his limbs.

'Think I'll just take a walk outside, get a breath of air,' he said. 'Why don't you come with me? It would do you good to get out of that chair.'

She gave him a look of crushing reproach. 'No, thank you.' Her reply was almost prim. 'I prefer to stay here.'

He hesitated. 'I haven't phoned Mum and Dad yet, I think I'll walk as far as the phone booth, they will have to be told.' Ann had returned her attention to the baby and made no answer to this. 'I might as well check the car while I'm out. Turn the engine over, like. Or else it won't start when we need it next, it's very cold for it to be standing.'

This too failed to draw comment from Ann and Philip studied the bent head as if to impress every detail on his memory before turning and leaving the room.

CHAPTER 14

Emerging from the hospital like some nocturnal creature newly come from its burrow, Philip stood blinking within the glow cast by the entrance lamps. It was cold out here, the frost nipped at his exposed skin and the artificial heat engendered by his long vigil indoors drained away, leaving him shivering in his inadequate lightweight suit. Shaking with both nerves and cold, he cursed himself for not having paused to put on his overcoat. Too late to go back for it now, he decided, he wanted to get the next few minutes over, for once he delayed he might never screw up the courage again.

Feeling like a bad amateur actor, he strode quickly across the hospital forecourt in the direction of the car-park, where he made great show of searching in all directions for the vehicle he knew to be miles away. Determined to play this part of the farce to its ultimate, he allowed his hurrying footsteps to break into a trot as he passed up and down the rows of parked cars before turning at last to the car-park attendant's hut. After hammering on the wooden door he hopped from one foot to the other, beating his arms against his body to instil some warmth into his shivering frame.

The attendant peered out at him and grunted something that might, or might not have been an enquiry.

'Sorry to bother you,' Philip told him through chattering teeth, 'but I can't seem to find my car.'

'Where'd yer leave it?'

'Just over there.' He waved an arm vaguely in the direction he'd once been parked.

'Have yer looked?'

'Of course I've looked.'

'Wait a minute.' The door was closed in his face, to be opened a few minutes later by the attendant who now had a top-coat and a muffler over his uniform. He brandished a large torch at Philip. 'What colour is it?'

'Er, green. A sort of lightish green. It's an old Morris.'

'Oh, is it. C'mon then, let's have a look.'

They walked up and down the lines of cars with Philip shaking his head dismissively each time the attendant paused to hold the torch beam on any car of a shade that might loosely be described as green. 'We-ell, yer'd better get the police, I should think,' the attendant said as they reached the last car in the line. 'That's if yer sure yer left it in this here car-park.'

'But aren't you going to do that? After all, it *is* part of your job, surely.' Philip injected a note of impatience into his voice, trying to make his portrayal of a man whose car had gone missing as realistic as possible. Besides, he really had thought the man would save him from this most uncomfortable part in his plans.

'My job is ter mek sure there's room fer folks ter get in and out of the car-park. Not ter chase after cars as ain't here. 'Sides, I ain't got no phone.' A note of injury crept into the man's voice over the omission of this most vital piece of equipment.

'Well, if that's the best you can do, I call it a poor tale! I'll get the police here myself and when I do you had better be ready to answer some questions.' By now Philip was so incensed at the man's uncompromising attitude his anger was genuine; and it wasn't until he found himself facing the desk-sergeant at the local police station that he paused to recollect his story was, in the main, purely fictitious.

'And, er, well that's all there is to say really,' he concluded lamely running out of both steam and conviction at once.

'Better wait here a minute if you don't mind.' The desk sergeant lifted the hinged counter-flap and stepped around it to Philip's side. 'I'll get someone to take a statement.' He crossed to a door at the rear of the room, opened it and poked his head through the gap. 'Oh, Jim —' his voice came back to Philip, muffled by the confines of the room— 'can you get a statement from this chappie out here? Say's he's lost his car.'

There was a long pause suggesting the exchange of some sort of silent confidence before a deliberately loud and casual voice replied, 'Right-e-o, Serge. Just show him through then, would you.'

The sergeant's head and shoulders reappeared and he beckoned to Philip. 'Care to step through here, please, sir.'

Philip did as he was bid and found himself in a very small room containing one metal filing cabinet, one battered desk with a straight-backed chair standing on either side, and one very large policeman who seemed to fill entirely any remaining space. Feeling decidedly nervous, he took the chair indicated and launched himself into his story for the second time.

The constable listened without interruption until he came to the end, then requested, 'Just let me get this straight. You have been at the hospital sitting with your wife and child since yesterday afternoon. Is that correct?'

'Yes . . . Er, no. No, not quite. I *did* go home this morning—early. My wife needed some things.'

'And how did you get home? By car?'

'No, oh no. I walked . . . I . . . I was too tired to drive . . . I walked.'

'Rather a tidy step, that. All the way from the General out to—where is it? Lynden Grove?'

'Yes, I know. But like I said, I was feeling too done up to drive.'

'And when did you last check on your car?'

'I didn't. Not check on it, that is. I parked it at the hospital some time yesterday afternoon. I'm not quite sure of the exact time—latish . . . it was getting dark. And I went to get it just now, and it was gone.' As he spoke he thrust his shaking hands deep into his pocket for fear their trembling should give him away. His fingers encountered the spiky metal of his car keys and he snatched them away in a panic of indecision. Would he be carrying the keys if his story was true? Could the fact that he still had them in his possession be made to incriminate him? Ought he to claim that he had left them in the car?

The policeman was watching him narrowly. 'What is it, sir? Something you've not told us?'

'I, er, no . . . It's the keys! I still have the keys.' Pulling them from his pocket, Philip almost threw them across the desk, realizing with a sudden upward surge of his spirits that far from incriminating him, they might even help substantiate his claims of theft. 'See. The car was locked when I left it.'

'I should certainly hope so,' the constable said heavily. 'Nobody with any sense leaves their car standing open these days. Now then, let's go over the whole thing once again if you don't mind, then I'll write it up and you will be free to go.'

'Thank you.' Philip swallowed convulsively, wishing above all else that he'd never embarked on this exercise. He should have left it to the police to come to him when they discovered his abandoned car, as they most surely would before very much longer.

Telling the story to Ann after his ordeal at the police station came as something of an anticlimax. She paid little attention to his tale, which he told with an assumed air of righteous indignation in a bid to stress his own innocence should any question be asked of her later. But he talked in vain, for the loss of their once fondly cherished old car meant nothing to her now and she allowed his words to wash over her without any display of interest. After a while she stirred, changed position in her chair and said dully, 'Why don't you go home, Philip? You can do nothing here.'

He flinched at this fresh evidence of her rejection. Did she have to make it so obvious that she didn't want him around? Well, if that was how she wanted it he'd be the last person to argue! The brief flash of anger died even as it was born and he paused to cast a glance that implored her for solace before the futility of such a hope sent him plodding down the hospital corridor towards the exit doors. Heedless now of the freezing temperatures, he turned his footsteps homewards, a sore pain in his heart cutting him off from all but his own misery.

He thought briefly of Dawn; she would be waiting to hear how things had gone. For a moment he was tempted to go to her, he had a great need of her staunch support, then he recalled that Trevor would be home and dismissed the idea. He had no wish to take him into his confidence regarding the Mottershead business and he couldn't face any more pretence — not today. So he continued his lonely journey to Lynden Grove.

It was well he did, for the barely suppressed angers that had been smouldering between Dawn and Trevor were in the course of full eruption about the time Philip wearily let himself in at his front door. The explosion had been triggered by an innocent question from three-year-old David, who, flushed and rosy from his pre-bedtime bath, begged his daddy to allow him 'just a bit more time,' in his company before being taken up to bed.

'Not tonight, old son.' Trevor scooped him up and tossed him skywards. Tonight your poor old dad's got a bone in his arm.'

'Oh, Daddy, please. Ple-eease.'

'Not another minute. Off to bed with you. I'm busy now.'

'Is Uncle Philip coming again? Is that why?' The piping treble held remnants of the excited laughter engendered by his impromptu flight.

Trevor gave him a playful shake. 'You young villain, it's any excuse to postpone the evil hour with you, isn't it? Your Uncle Philip hasn't been to see us since before we moved in, so why should you expect him tonight in particular?'

'He has, Daddy. He has. He came today and —'

'Stop shaking him about and get him off to bed.' Dawn

cut hastily across her son's confidences as Trevor froze into a wary stillness. He turned, David in his arms, to subject her to a silent, half-accusing scrutiny. 'He came to tell me about the baby.' Guilt over her involvement in Philip's secret stained her cheeks and she defended herself against the look in Trevor's eye with an unnecessary vigour that served only to create further suspicion.

'Say good night, Davy,' Trevor said slowly, his eyes never leaving Dawn's face. 'Come along, Mark. You can go up now too.' Any protest his eldest may have made remained unspoken as the child, catching sight of his father's grim face, rose from his crossed-leg position immediately in front of the television set and went to join his brother.

After tucking David into his bed Trevor turned to do the same for Mark and was about to switch out the light on his way out of their bedroom when David sat up, throwing his bedclothes aside as he asked in a sing-song, teasing voice, 'Can you guess a secret, Daddy?'

'Not tonight, son. You lie down now and go to sleep.'

'It's about Uncle Philip.' The child glowed with importance.

Trevor sighed deeply. 'All right then, what is it?'

Something in his tone checked David's bubbling humour and he hesitated, pretending a sudden interest in his pyjama buttons.

Trevor was inclined to let it go but some demon halted him as he reached the bedroom door and made him persist. 'Come on, Davy. You have to tell me now.'

The child looked at him under lowered brows, then gasped in a rush of confusion, 'I saw Uncle Philip kissing my mummy,' as he shot beneath the bedclothes. He kept them pulled over his head until he was sure enough time had elapsed for his father to have quit the room.

'What did you have to say that for?' his brother asked crossly as he poked up for air. 'You're just stupid, you are.'

'Oh no I'm not. I *did* see them kissing, so there!'

In the room below, man and wife stared at each other, their faces set and hostile. 'Are you going to tell me about it or do I have to hear it all from the boy?' There was that in Trevor's voice which hinted she stood already condemned and Dawn's hot temper thrust aside a reasonable, confiding explanation that might yet have saved their relationship.

'Tell you about what? I don't know what you mean.' How much had David overheard? And more to the point, how much had he repeated?

'Oh, you know all right. Don't make it strange. Butler didn't come simply to tell you about the baby, did he? There's the telephone for that.'

Dawn eyed him narrowly. If she told him the truth, which way would he jump?

'Answer me, damn you.'

Rage that he should dare use that tone pushed aside all caution and she rounded on him prepared to do battle. 'Who the hell do you think you are talking to?'

'I'm talking to you. I want to know what's going on here.'

'Going on? Going on? Use your bloody senses, man. What do you think is going on?'

'Pretty obvious isn't it? I don't really know why I bothered to ask.' Some of his anger died as he stared at her, a mixture of hurt and resentment in his eyes. 'He told me, Dawn . . . Our David.'

Futile irritation over her own neglect mingled with an anxious desire to preserve Philip's alibi at all costs. Why hadn't she thought to check on David's whereabouts before Philip said too much. She should have known that young monkey wouldn't miss a thing. 'David?' she began, hastily trying to cobble some story together that Trevor might be persuaded to accept.

'David. Our son. Our three-year-old son.'

Her temper rose afresh at this pedantic speech. 'I am

perfectly aware how old our son is, thank you. So what else are you rabbiting about?'

'Rabbiting, am I? Is that what you call it when a child of his age tells me he has seen his mother kissing another man?'

'Kissing . . . ?' Dawn stared at him in amazement. Surely that wasn't what this was all about? That chaste little peck?

Too entrenched in the green trough of jealousy to notice her expression harden, Trevor ground on, 'How long has he been coming here? Since we moved, is it? My God!' A new sword pierced him and he went on to his utter destruction. 'No wonder you wanted to stay on in Lynden Grove. You must have been knocking on with him even then.'

Dawn gasped under the shock of this accusation and was momentarily silenced. Then a consuming rage took her, shaking her from head to toe. Fingers hooked into claws, she glared at him, a raking, scathing glance designed to shrivel him where he stood. 'You bastard! You lousy, rotten, undersized little shit! So you think I'm having it away with Philip, do you? Well, let me tell you, I just wish I was. To have myself a real man after being shackled to you . . . Dear God, how I wish I was having it away with him.' A passionate desire to wound drove her on. 'Here!' She snatched the evening paper from the side of her chair and thrust it at him. 'This is the affair I've been having. Banner headlines, why don't you read them.' She rattled the paper savagely and Trevor reached to take it from her, his eyes fixed on hers, unable to tear them away from the contempt he saw there. For a second he stood clutching the crumpled news-sheets without being aware that he did so, then he lowered his eyes to scan the front page.

'What am I supposed to be looking at?' he asked, sub-dued by the force of his wife's rage.

'These — the headlines. They're plenty big enough, I would have thought, even for a man blinded by passion.'

'There is no need for sarcasm, Dawn. I am just at a loss to understand what they have to do with you and Butler. "Hit and run victim in coma," ' he read aloud. ' "No details of identity yet disclosed." How can this have any bearing on you and him?'

'The victim they refer to is Mottershead. Kevin Mottershead. *The* Kevin Mottershead of Lynden Grove fame.'

'Mottershead? An affair? But . . . but I . . . Oh no! No, Dawn . . .' A new and even more sickening thought beset him. 'You . . . You're not . . . not . . .'

'Give me strength.' Dawn rolled her eyes skywards. 'As you so rightly say, my dear, No, I am not. Try not to be any more idiotic than you can help. How would I be having any sort of affair with a lout like that? What am I, do you think? All I'm trying to tell you is that Philip has obliged us all by doing what the rest of you lacked the guts for . . . He ran him down! And that's why he came here today.'

'Ran him . . . You don't mean. Philip deliberately . . .' He couldn't finish the sentence. Shock and disbelief wiped the hurt from his face as he took in the details of the newspaper story. 'It says here, car driver being sought by the police. He can't hope . . . He'll never . . . Lord, Dawn. This is terrible.'

'Terrible? What's so terrible about it? I think what he did deserves a medal. What I can't understand is why it took him so long.'

'You can't really mean that.'

'Oh yes I do. And what's more, I'll do everything in my power to help him get away with it.'

'Not if I have any say in the matter, you won't.'

'But you're not going to have any say, are you? What business is it of yours? You haven't the guts to do what Philip did, nor ever would have. Not even if it was one of your own kids Mottershead had maimed.'

'No, I wouldn't have the guts, as you put it. Nor would I have the inclination. Neither do I have the inclination to shelter Philip in this. If he doesn't go to the police, then I will.'

'*What?*' The word was a screech of outrage. 'What did you say, you—you—jumped-up-never-come-down-two-faced insufferable prig.' She advanced on Trevor, her face suffused with anger. 'Don't you dare even to suggest turning him in or I'll kill you.'

'Don't say any more, Dawn. You've gone far enough now.' His figure, dwarfed by her rage, was tensed, his face carried a warning.

'Why, you bastard!' Beside herself now, Dawn struck out at him, her fingers connecting with a neck-jarring slap across the side of his face. He caught at her hand, his grip on her wrist hard and uncaring, his fingers bit deep into her flesh as he exerted his strength to hold her still. Vivid red wheals rose across the white flesh above the line of his beard, and they stood toe to toe reading hatred and disgust in each others' eyes.

'I've finished with you, Dawn. I've had enough. I'll leave just as soon as I've packed but I'll be back for the children,' he promised quietly.

'Then piss off! And don't think I'll stand in your way when it comes to the kids. You can have them! And all the rest that goes with them so don't think you'll hit back at me through them. Go on, sod off! Get out, you bloody worm!' She wrenched herself away from his grasp and went to fling open the door.

Trevor gave her just one pitying glance as he passed on his way out, all thoughts of a dignified exit extinguished by her obvious haste to see him go. Once outside, the slam of the front door still ringing in his ears, he paused locked in indecision. Here he was, in the bitter cold of a winter's night, clad only in a light indoor sweater, trousers and carpet slippers. He had no money in his pockets, the car keys and his wallet were in the house behind him along with the remains of the past ten years of his life. Where did he go from here? He and Dawn were unquestionably through. He would never go back after the taunts which had stripped him of both his pride and his manhood, he could never forgive her for the things she had said. But he had meant what he said about the children, he would have them if he had to drag her name through every court in the land in order to get them. That resolve gave him purpose and he recalled the spare set of keys taped to the inside of the front bumper. He would drive himself over to his father's place and ask if he might stay there while he got himself sorted out. The old man lived alone since Trevor and his sisters had married, their mother having died many years ago, so there should be room enough for him.

Shivering now, both from reaction to the recent stormy scene and the cold, he groped along the muddy recess behind the car bumper and located the keys. The car started at the first turn and he backed carefully into the road and drove off without caring to look back for any twitch of the closed curtains which might indicate that Dawn was watching him go.

Changing up through the gears as he increased speed, he promised himself that he would be back for his children as soon as possible. In the meantime . . . In the meantime, he would have to swallow his pride and beg shelter from his dad. And on his way there, he'd stop off at Lynden Grove just long enough to advise Philip Butler that unless he gave himself up to the police he, Trevor Austin, would do the job for him!

CHAPTER 15

The doorbell echoed stridently but failed to rouse Philip from his morose, inward study; not until George resorted to a hefty knocking was he brought to answer the door.

'Thought you'd gone deaf,' his neighbour greeted him bluntly. 'How are things?'

'Much the same.' Philip led the way into the lounge and lifted a whisky bottle from a side table in silent invitation.

George nodded acceptance. 'I only came to tell you the latest,' he said as he took the generously filled glass. 'Sue reckons there have been ructions at the Knights'. Joan told her . . . Hey, Joan, You know, Joan—Harry's missus,' he pressed with jocular emphasis at Philip's apparent failure to give his imminent disclosure due importance. Then, having successfully captured his host's attention, he proceeded with enthusiasm, 'Well, it seems she delivered Harry an ultimatum after the court case. It was a straight down the middle "me or that bitch" thing, and poor old Harry's had to toe the line ever since. Now it appears, though we can't be certain, mind you, it appears that young Christine and that Mottershead bloke have been shacked up together since he got out. Harry knew nothing about it until his ex-wife rang his home some time today. *And*, listen to this, Joan—took—the—call!' George brought the information out like a rabbit from a hat.

Philip's expression had sharpened at the mention of Mottershead's name and he now prompted impatiently, 'Go on.'

Thoroughly enjoying himself, George continued. 'She was having kittens—Harry's missus. The ex, I mean, not Joan. Although, come to think of it—'

'George, for God's sake!'

'Sorry.' He had the grace to look contrite and hurriedly condensed the rest of his story in an effort to make amends. 'What it boils down to is this: Christine went screaming round to her mother after seeing the piece about your trouble in this morning's rag. Lover-boy has taken off on his toes, it seems, and she's scared stiff that she's been left to carry the can. Kept on about it being an accident, he hadn't meant no kid to get hurt, and all that jazz. Well, Joan rounded on Harry like it was his fault, with the result that he's gone charging over to his ex-wife's like a knight to the rescue—Oh, that's a good one—Harry Knight, knight to the rescue— . . . Oh, well. Please yourself.' George shrugged and went on with his story. 'Joan says Christine is claiming she knew nothing about the business with the firework until today. She's in a blue funk now and ready to shop Mottershead for running out on her.' He punched Philip's shoulder. 'You've got him this time, Phil. Really got him. They'll turn the key on him for good after this little lot. And not before time, if you want my opinion.'

Philip studied George curiously, recalling that he had seemed to extract equal enjoyment out of Mottershead's threats to himself at the time of the court hearing. 'You should have been around at the time of the gladiators, George,' he said dampeningly.

'Thanks very much.'

Philip shrugged and rubbed his unshaven jaw, feeling too emotionally battered to engage in further aggravation. 'No offence, George. It's just . . . You know.'

' 'Sall right. I can see you are pretty much all in. Just thought you'd like to know, though.' He placed his now empty glass on the side table and went through the motions of taking his leave.

'Yeah, sure. Thanks for coming.' Philip made no attempt to delay his departure and returned to the lounge after seeing him out to refill his own glass and mull over the bitter irony of his situation. Christine was going to the police. Mottershead would have got his deserts in any event . . . When the doorbell pealed for the second time that evening he was asking himself why the hell he had ever interfered.

It wasn't until he'd found himself pulling in to the kerb outside the familiar house on Lynden Grove that Trevor paused to examine the motives responsible for bringing him there. He had never really intended to turn Philip in, nor did he mean to push him into making a confession, but the deep hurt and damaged pride he'd sustained in his wife's scathing attack goaded him into lashing out in return. It didn't have to be his own tormentor who suffered — anyone would do — just so long as he had company in this present state of misery. It was in full recognition of this that he'd climbed out of his car and gone to lean on Philip Butler's doorbell. After all, Philip was in some part responsible for the majority of Dawn's invectives, he was telling himself righteously as the door opened.

The sight of his friend's haunted face gave Trevor pause; did he really want to go on with this? Then Philip moved forward as he recognized his caller, a mask almost cunning in its disarming openness replacing his former unguarded expression, turning his attempts at a welcoming smile into a smug leer in Trevor's eyes and killing forever his burgeoning sympathy.

'Hello, Trev. What brings you here?' Only by a slight tremor did his voice betray the shock he'd experienced at seeing his former neighbour.

'I have to talk to you. Can we go inside?'

'Sorry. I wasn't thinking.' He beckoned Trevor over the threshold. 'I've had so much on my mind.'

'Not least of which would be Kevin Mottershead, I should hope.'

Philip pushed the door closed and sagged forward, pressing his forehead to its cool surface. He kept his back turned towards Trevor. 'Dawn told you then,' he said in a voice scarcely above a whisper.

'Of course she told me! Did you think she wouldn't? Did you think she was so besotted with you she would pass up the opportunity for a bit of juicy gossip? Damn you, man, why don't you look at me?' Trevor caught at the averted shoulder and Philip turned round to stare down at him.

Stark primeval passion flashed between them, feelings too raw and deep to be defined as civilized held them within an ace of falling upon each other in deadly combat. Philip was first to shift his gaze. Exhausted to the point of automation, he allowed his eyes to fall and noticed for the first time the flaming brand Dawn's fingers had left across Trevor's face.

'What on earth have you—' he began, then checked his tongue, aware still of the bristling animosity in the other man's attitude.

Of a sudden that aggressive emotion dissolved, leaving Trevor staring ruefully up at the taller man. 'Philip, I'm sorry.' He extended his hand and when Philip took it after only a moment's hesitation, he cupped his other hand about it in a gesture of friendship. 'I don't know what's come over me,' he said, shaking his head. 'And that's not true either,' he added quickly. 'I've walked out on Dawn. She . . . I . . . we'll get a divorce, I suppose.' He fingered his right cheek.

'Divorce? Look, Trev, come and have a drink. Let's talk about this.'

'No. No, I won't, thanks. I have to drive over to my dad's and the way I feel now one drink would have me legless.'

'Well, come and sit down at least, tell me about it. It's not . . . not really through any fault of mine, is it?' He watched Trevor's face anxiously.

'Could be.' Trevor shrugged. 'Could be that this would have happened sooner or later in any case. But it was Dawn's attitude over this business with Mottershead that finally sparked it off . . . Look here, Philip. You can't possibly hope to get away with it, you know. You have to go to the police.'

'Why? Because your marriage went down under the knock? Bit of getting your own back, is it?' The bristling undercurrent swirled momentarily to ruffle the surface of friendship between the two men.

'No, not now. It began like that I'll admit. I wanted to smack it in your teeth. But now . . . Oh, come on, Phil. You can't live with that on your conscience. Besides, when he comes round he's going to drop you in it anyway. So it would be better—'

'Comes round? How d'you mean, comes round?'

'Comes out of the coma. Haven't you read the papers? No, I can see you haven't. He's not dead,. Philip.'

Silence hung between them as Philip strove to analyse what the revelation could mean to him on so many counts. 'I don't know whether I'm glad or sorry,' he said at last. 'I wanted to kill him. Wanted to wipe out his very existence. Now . . . I just don't know. George was here. George Turner.' He eyed his former friend dubiously, wondering whether to tell all he'd learned.

'And?' Trevor prompted, sensing Philip's indecision.

'Oh, nothing much. He . . . Nothing. It was nothing.' The time for shared confidences between them was past and he let it go.

'What does Ann feel about it?' asked Trevor deliberately.

'Ann? Christ! I haven't told her—use your head.'

'But she'll find out. She's bound to, and then what?'

Philip shrank visibly as he replied, 'I suppose I'll have to tell her . . . some time. At least I can break it to her better than the police or whatever. Maybe she'll . . .' His voice trailed away.

'Yes. Well, maybe she will at that,' Trevor said for want of any more helpful remark. 'I think perhaps I'd better get off now. I'm sorry things have gone the way they have, Phil. For both of us.' He opened the front door and shuddered as the cold air licked his thinly clad body. 'I . . . hope the baby will come through okay . . . And Ann . . . And, well, I won't shop you if you decide not to go to the law.'

Philip made no reply. He was already living through the nightmare of the forthcoming scene with his wife, and Trevor let himself out without another word.

Ann's immediate reaction to her husband's confession was tempered somewhat by the sleepless hours she had spent in desperate prayer by her baby's cot. She received the news quietly, confounding Philip's preconceived notion that it would drive her into a fit of screaming hysterics. He had arrived at the hospital early the day following Trevor's visit, to find Ann pacing the corridor outside the intensive care unit, and had learned in response to his anxious enquiry that the specialist was making what he termed a routine examination of Melanie Jane. Relieved to hear that the child was holding her own, he had plunged straight into his story, afraid that the chance to tell it would be lost forever should he delay. He made as light as he could of the actual circumstances, passing rapidly on to excuse his actions in the light of his mental state at the time it occurred.

'I had to do it, Ann. I couldn't help myself. There he was, free as air, sound in limb and body, while . . . while our little girl . . . I wanted to *smash* him.' He thumped his right fist into the palm of his left in graphic demonstration.

'So I gather.' Ann's voice was low-pitched and perfectly controlled. 'And did you feel better for it? Did smashing him mend Melanie's hurts? Did it make everything right?'

'Oh Ann, Ann. Don't look at me like that.' He tried to

take her into his arms but she pulled away.

'How would you have me look at you? In starry-eyed admiration?' Her voice grew wilder now and more shrill. 'Let me tell you this, Philip. I don't admire you. I don't admire what you have done any more than I admire what that—that animal did to Melanie. And I don't think I will be able to forgive either of you, not if I live forever.'

'I'm sorry you're taking that line, Ann. I did what I did as much for you as for me.'

'No! Don't! Don't you dare lay the blame for this monstrous thing at my door. I didn't ask you to turn executioner. What you have done makes you no better than Mottershead and I don't care how you try to live with it, only don't try to make me your accomplice.'

'Ann, please, I love you. And I love Melanie. Don't class me with that swine.'

'You've left it to late to ask that, Philip. I don't think I'll ever be able to look at you again without remembering what you have done.' She stared at him, a long, hard stare of condemnation.

'I see . . . Then there really is nothing left for us . . . Not if that's true. I've felt us drifting apart ever since this thing happened. I knew . . . I knew I had lost you yesterday, but I couldn't help hoping . . .' Philip waited, hoping Ann would relent, but she didn't alter her gaze, not in all the long time it took for her to make her way past him in the narrow corridor.

'I'll give myself up, Ann. I'll go to the police, tell them it was me.' He grabbed at her arm, wanting to keep her close, to hold on to this their final moment.

Ann prised his fingers from her arm. 'I don't care what you do, nor who you tell. Just let me go, that's all I ask.'

'But, Ann . . . I might go to prison . . . Years . . . You can't say you don't care.' He was pleading now, begging her for understanding.

The hard light died from her eyes and they filled with

tears. 'All I care about is Melanie Jane. She is the end result of your type of caring. You've destroyed whatever there might have been in the future for us just as surely as Mottershead and maggots like him destroy any chance of ordinary people coming together as friends. Go to the police, Philip. Tell them what you have done. Then see if you can put it right!'

The bitterness underlying her words cut Philip to the bone. He knew he would hear them again and again, they would intrude on his memories, cancel the warmth from tender recollections and rob him of peace of mind to the end of his days. He watched Ann start back along the corridor towards her cell-like room before he turned on his heel and made for the exit.

This wasn't the way he'd pictured things in that other lifetime when he and Ann had first learned she was pregnant. When they had lived happily side by side with neighbours in a close little community that cared one for the other, when vandals were things that crawled from under stones in somebody else's backyard, when he and Trevor and George and Harry were neighbours, drinking partners, yarn swappers and friends. Where had it all gone? *When* had it all gone? Not when the vandals first came. Not when they had joined together to rid themselves of those hell-hounds. Then when?

When you caught their disease and set out to humiliate and degrade, came the mocking inner voice. When neighbour turned against neighbour because of a fault in their midst. When you forsook tolerance in favour of revenge. Faster and faster whirled the accusing dervish. Dawn and Trevor, Harry, Christine and Joan. Ann and he—and Melanie. Yes, Melanie . . . And Mottershead, came the voice that refused to be silenced, don't forget about him.

The pavement rang under his heels as Philip headed resolutely across town towards the police station driven by the cruel goad of regret. As he neared the forbidding grey

building his thoughts turned to the problem in hand and
his need to gain clemency for his share of the blame.
Maybe, once they knew why he'd done what he did,
maybe they would take a lenient view. After all, Mottershead wasn't dead, and once he'd told them about Melanie
Jane, once they'd looked through their records and confirmed his story with Christine's . . . Well, they'd have to
see his side of it, surely. The police force were human,
they'd be half way in his favour when they learned how
much of a villain his hit-and-run victim had been. Trevor
had said the man's identity was not known, or not disclosed, hadn't he? Well, he'd disclose it for them now . . .
Then they'd see.

He strode on, his long legs rapidly covering the ground
to bring him outside the old grey stone building. He
halted at the foot of the entrance steps, going over his
story again in his mind, deciding on the best way to tell it.

Ann had no idea of the passage of time, she had stumbled
into the little curtained-off room seeking refuge from the
thought of Philip deliberately driving his car at a fellow
human being. Slumped on the bed, her face buried in her
hands, she tried to push the grisly picture out of her
mind. Philip's face narrowed in hate, a vague outline of
the other man, Mottershead, as he fell under the spinning
wheels, beat back at her from her closed eyelids. A hand,
firm but kindly fell on her shoulder. She opened her eyes
reluctantly. What fresh trouble awaited now?

'Mrs. Butler.' The nurse spoke her name softly. 'You
have been told, then?'

'Told?' she asked wonderingly. How could this girl have
heard already?

'About the baby?'

The baby! Ann shot to her feet, knocking the kindly
hand aside. 'No. No I haven't. What is it about the baby?'
she asked wildly.

'Sit down, dear. Sit down. It isn't good news, I'm afraid.' Pressure was applied to push Ann back to the bed and she sank down unresisting now as she guessed what must come next.

'She slipped away a few minutes ago . . . The doctor was with her . . . She didn't suffer . . . She never came round.'

Ann stared at the fragment of polished floor close to her feet. How clean it was. How bright, and how beautifully clean.

'Mrs. Butler.'

She heard the nurse speak her name and thought crossly; why doesn't she keep quiet? Can't she see I'm busy . . . I have to look at this lovely floor.

'Mrs. Butler. Would you like to lie down, dear? I'll get you something that will help.'

Ann raised her eyes and studied the nurse's face. How could she be so silly? What could she or anyone possibly get that would help her now? Philip was gone. Hadn't she dispensed with his affections almost as wantonly as he had dispensed with Mottershead, and now . . . Now, Melanie Jane. They had both gone. She was past any help this girl could offer. She climbed to her feet an old, old woman. Without faltering, she stepped out of the cubicle and started along the echoing corridor. Where it met a similar corridor running off to the right she stepped without hesitation directly into the path of the two women emerging from its mouth. The impact of their collision rocked her back on her heels and had it not been for the younger of the two who shot out a hand to steady her, she would have fallen.

'Why it's—it's Ann, isn't it?'

Vaguely Ann recalled the young girl's face. Wasn't she something to do with Philip?

'Helen. Helen Broadhurst.' The girl herself supplied the answer. 'I . . . I heard about the baby, Ann . . . How is she?' There was a frightening quality about the face staring back at her that made her go on. 'Is Philip here? Is he with you?'

Ann moved her head in a negative gesture.

'Then can we help? This is my mother.' She drew the older woman closer with a little protective movement.

Ann's eyes travelled slowly to take in this newcomer. Had she been more herself she would have recognized at once the dreadful acceptance of loss on that tear-stained face. As it was, she barely realized the third presence. 'Did you want Philip?' she asked suddenly as one child might ask another if it wanted a sweet.

'No, Ann. No . . . we're here . . . we came to see Stephen.' The girl swallowed painfully. 'My brother . . . He was knocked down . . . Hit and run . . .' Then, because it seemed safer to pursue her own grief than to probe the one she sensed emanating from the stricken figure before her, she went on hesitantly, 'He was a policeman, you know. He was . . . he was coming off duty early the day before yesterday, when . . . when . . .'

'Policeman? Coming off duty?' Ann prattled.

'Yes.' Helen recovered herself and tightened her arm comfortingly about her mother. 'He was in the CID working with the drugs squad. We . . . the police think . . . they think since he was undercover, dressed like a hippie, they think it may have been a deliberate killing. We . . . we didn't know, we weren't told . . . Not till a few hours ago . . . He was wearing my ear-ring.' The girl's strangled sob robbed the incongruous remark of its strangeness. She bit back her tears and went on, 'It happened here . . . in town. He was crossing . . .' Her voice faded to a whisper, leaving the horror of her loss hanging in the clinical air of the hospital corridor.

'Shush, love. Shhh. I'm sure your friend has enough troubles without listening to ours.' Their roles were reversed now and it was Helen's mother who had the supportive one.

She turned a look of apprehension towards Ann's tormented face. Poor soul, she seemed to have taken their grief to herself, and by the looks of her she was about at the end of her tether. She squeezed her daughter's hand, trying to warn her to keep silent, afraid lest she disturb this poor girl even further.

She need not have worried. The light behind the brown eyes had dimmed a little with Helen's every word until now they held nothing but darkness. Ann was already dwelling in safe, deep and eternal night, with no dreams to haunt the sleeper.